Even though s... it pretty clear ... was leaving he... a chance to change her mind.

She could pull back and put on the brakes. No harm. No foul. Or she could plough full steam ahead.

Lara didn't feel reckless when she chose the latter. Rather, she felt right.

"Your shirt. I've been wondering what you would look like without it."

Deep laughter rumbled again. With his body still pressed against hers, she felt his mirth as much as she heard it. The sensation was oddly erotic, but what had the breath backing up in her lungs was his reply.

"I've been wondering the same thing. What do you say we both satisfy our curiosity?"

Dear Reader

I'm no gourmet chef, but I'm a pretty decent cook—especially when I'm not on a deadline for a book. My husband and kids will tell you the closer I get to turning in a manuscript, the more pizza and cereal they wind up eating for supper!

Even though my culinary skills may be mediocre, I love watching cooking programmes. I am especially addicted to competitions such as The Food Network's *Iron Chef* and *Chopped!* So when I decided to write a book that featured a couple of talented chefs who have the hots for each other, I figured what better way to ratchet up the heat than to pit them against each other on a televised cooking contest?

Lara Durham and Finn Westbrook both have compelling reasons for wanting to win the show and the executive chef position at a New York landmark restaurant that goes with it. Those reasons become major obstacles, of course, when they start to fall in love.

Bon appétit!

Jackie Braun

FALLING FOR
HER RIVAL

BY
JACKIE BRAUN

Published in Great Britain 2014
by Mills & Boon, an imprint of Harlequin (UK) Limited,
Eton House, 18-24 Paradise Road, Richmond, Surrey, TW9 1SR

© 2014 Jackie Braun Fridline

ISBN: 978 0 263 91137 4

Harlequin (UK) Limited's policy is to use papers that are natural, renewable and recyclable products and made from wood grown in sustainable forests. The logging and manufacturing processes conform to the legal environmental regulations of the country of origin.

Printed and bound in Spain
by Blackprint CPI, Barcelona

Jackie Braun is the author of more than two dozen romance novels. She is a three-times RITA® Award finalist, a four-time National Readers' Choice Awards finalist, the winner of a Rising Star Award in traditional romantic fiction and was nominated for Series Storyteller of the Year by *RT Book Reviews* in 2008. She lives in Michigan with her husband and two sons, and can be reached through her website at www.jackiebraun.com

Other Modern Tempted™ titles by Jackie Braun:

AFTER THE PARTY

This and other titles by Jackie Braun are available in eBook format from www.millsandboon.co.uk

With much love to my husband and boys for their support.

CHAPTER ONE

Gather ingredients

LARA DUNHAM MOVED the sprig of basil a fraction of an inch to the left on a sautéed chicken breast that sat atop a bed of risotto and asparagus tips. Afterward, she took a step back. Standing shoulder to shoulder with the food editor of *Home Chef* magazine, she eyed the table.

"I don't know," the other woman murmured. "It still doesn't look right."

Nor did it taste right, but Lara kept the thought to herself. She'd filched a nibble during the setup. It wasn't merely a trick of the trade that had left her palate dissatisfied. Food used in photo shoots was often undercooked to help retain moisture. No, in this case, the rice needed more seasoning. In fact, it needed *a lot* more seasoning. But she bit her tongue because doctoring up the recipes wasn't her call.

She did say, "The square plate isn't working for me."

Just as she'd suspected, it was giving off a decidedly Asian vibe that didn't lend itself to the Italian-inspired dish.

The plate had been the editor's suggestion; one Lara had taken out of expediency rather than agreement. She knew from past experience with the prickly older woman that it was easier and ultimately less time-consuming to show her that something didn't work than to insist on something else up front.

Sure enough, the editor made a humming sound before agreeing. Lara held back a triumphant smile and turned to the college intern who was assisting her.

"Bring me the large round one with the wide rim. And let's swap out the candles and napkin rings." Again, they had been the older woman's suggestion. "The silver is too formal."

Forty-five minutes later, with the food carefully replated and the tablescape tweaked to represent Lara's vision, the photographer got his shot. It would grace the October cover of the national publication and be seen by millions of people.

"Another fabulous shoot," the editor gushed as the photographer gathered up his equipment and Lara prepared to leave the magazine's offices. "I should know better than to give you suggestions. What you come up with always looks better. No one makes food look more appetizing than you do."

Lara accepted the compliment with a nod. As a food stylist, that was her job and she was good at it. She was much sought after because of her attention to detail, a reputation that she'd earned over the course of nearly a decade.

Perhaps that was why it stung so badly that to her father, Lara remained a colossal disappointment.

Those who can, cook. Those who can't, style food.

So sayeth the legendary restaurateur Clifton Chesterfield.

He'd paid her tuition to the top-rated culinary school in the country, after which he'd sent her abroad for two years to study cooking techniques in both Tuscany and the south of France. From the time Lara had been old enough to make a simple roux, his plan had been that she would follow in his footsteps and someday run the kitchen at the New York landmark that bore his name. The landmark where he'd spent practically every waking hour of Lara's childhood.

Was it any wonder that she'd resented the restaurant? Was it any wonder that she'd resented him for choosing it over his family?

So, as a full-of-herself young twentysomething, she'd rebelled. And she'd done so spectacularly.

At thirty-three, Lara could look back and admit that she'd taken her revolt too far. She'd publicly dissed both her father and his beloved restaurant, and then married the only food critic in Manhattan who'd ever dared to give the Chesterfield a subpar rating.

Her marriage to Jeffrey Dunham had lasted only slightly longer than the rise on a first-year culinary student's soufflé before she'd come to her senses. By then, however, the damage was done. Her father refused to speak to her.

Six years later, Lara was old enough and wise enough to admit that she'd cut off her nose to spite her face. Irony of ironies, she now wanted to hang up her stylist credentials and pursue a career as a chef. She also wanted her dad's respect, if not his affection. She wanted to hear him say, "Well-done."

But when she'd approached him a year earlier about a job, he'd broken his silence only long enough to refuse to hire her—not even to do prep work. And since *he* wouldn't hire her, no credible kitchen in the city would either. Such was Clifton Chesterfield's reach and reputation.

Well, finally, she had an opportunity to make her father see her as a serious chef, and Lara wasn't about to blow it.

With the shoot wrapped, she stepped outside to catch a cab. Barring a traffic tie-up, she had just enough time to make it to Midtown before one o'clock. Of course, she wouldn't have a chance to grab lunch, but since nerves had tied her stomach in knots, she wasn't complaining.

Overhead, fat clouds the color of ripe eggplants were huddled together. Any moment, the sky was going to open up and it was going to pour, and she hadn't brought an umbrella. She tried not to think of the weather as a bad omen, but she couldn't deny its effect on her hair, which had a hard enough time holding a curl when there was no humidity. It was stick straight now, a glossy auburn curtain that fell even with her shoulders. Before raising her arm to hail a cab, she fussed with the fringe of bangs she already regretted getting at her last salon visit.

When a taxi pulled to a stop a moment later, she dashed for it. She reached for the door handle at the same time a man did. Their fingers brushed and they both stepped back.

"Oh!" Lara gasped, not only because she had competition for the ride, but because the competition in question was drop-dead gorgeous.

While most of the men on the street at this time of the day wore decked-out business attire, carrying briefcases and barking orders into cell phones, this one was wearing faded jeans and a lightweight windbreaker. He looked as if he should have a surfboard tucked under his arm and be heading out to Long Beach to catch a wave. His face was tanned. His hair was a sandy-brown with streaks of sun-bleached blond thrown in. A quarter-inch worth of stubble shadowed his jaw and framed an easygoing smile that seemed at odds with his intense gray eyes.

"Rock, Paper, Scissors?" he asked.

"Why not?" she replied, hoping the rain would continue to hold off while they played.

"On the count of three, then."

She hiked the strap of her purse onto her shoulder to free up her hands and nodded.

"One. Two. Three," they said in unison as they each pounded a fist into the opposite palm.

Afterward he was holding his right hand out flat. Lara, meanwhile, was mimicking a cutting motion with her index and middle fingers.

"Scissors cut paper," she said unnecessarily.

With a shake of his head, the man said, "I had you figured for a rock."

Hmm. How to take that?

"Sorry to disappoint you."

"I wouldn't say I'm disappointed."

He held open the cab's door for her. Before closing it, however, he leaned inside. Something in his expression had changed so that it now matched the intensity in his eyes.

"Hey, since you're costing me my ride, can I…can I ask you for a favor?"

"I guess so," she said slowly. It wasn't wariness she felt exactly. More like anticipation. Like a kid on Christmas, getting ready to unwrap the last gift from beneath the tree.

But then he shook his head. "Nah. Forget it. Crazy," she thought he muttered as he started to straighten.

She tugged him back by saying, "No. Really. Ask. It's the least I can do."

He hesitated only a moment. "I'm on my way to something important. It's kind of a big deal for me. A game changer."

"A job interview?"

"Yeah. In a manner of speaking."

She nodded, understanding. So was she. In a manner of speaking. "So, what's the favor?"

"Can I…?" His gaze lowered to her lips. "Can I have a kiss for luck?"

Lara's breath whooshed out on a laugh even as parts of her body started to tingle. "I'll give you props for creativity. That's a line I've never heard before."

The man pinched his eyes closed, looking both self-conscious and alarmingly delicious. "Yeah. Pathetic. Forget it."

He started to straighten a second time. In another moment he would be closing the door, beyond her reach, and she would be on her way. Luck? What the heck? Lara figured she could use a little of it herself. And what would a kiss from a total stranger hurt, really? In a city that boasted more than eight million people, it wasn't as if she would run into him again. So, before he could retreat or she could entertain second thoughts, she grabbed the front of his jacket and hauled him to her.

Their lips bumped clumsily before settling in place. His were firm, the pressure sweet. She expected him to pull back afterward. Mission accomplished. That would be that. She would be on her way. But one of his hands came up. His palm cradled her jaw. The pad of his thumb stroked her cheek. Long fingers tangled in the hair over her ear. A pair of smoky eyes closed as a sigh escaped. His breath was a feather-soft caress on her face. When his mouth dived back in for seconds, she was grateful to be seated since her world tilted on its axis.

"Hey, buddy. You gettin' in or what?" the cabbie asked in a voice edged with impatience.

It served as a wet blanket to the unexpected bonfire that had flared inside Lara. The man eased away, his smile crooked and slightly self-conscious.

She felt the same way. Public displays of affection really weren't her thing.

"Nah. The lady won the cab fair and square," he said as he straightened.

"Good luck," Lara told him, reaching out to give his fingers a squeeze.

"Thanks." He studied their linked hands a moment. "You know, I don't think I'm going to need it after all."

Afterward, he closed the door and gave the cab's roof a thump with the same hand that had slid along her jaw. He was no longer smiling when the car pulled away. In fact, he was shaking his head, his gaze on the pavement. But he looked more bemused than annoyed, even as the heavens opened up and Mother Nature wrung out her wash.

It was with an effort that Lara regrouped. It wouldn't do to be distracted by hot lip-locks with even hotter strangers. She needed to be focused, fearless. She caught her reflection in the rearview mirror. What she looked was frazzled, flushed and a bit dazed. Her hair was mussed, her lip gloss long gone. Still, she considered the pleasure that had the corners of her mouth curving to be a pretty fair exchange for her disheveled state.

She pulled out her compact and used the drive time to touch up her makeup. Aside from lip gloss, she didn't wear very much, but given the long hours she spent indoors, a little blush on her pale cheeks was a must. The second swipe of mascara she added to her lashes helped keep her eyes from looking tired, even though she had slept poorly the night before.

Nerves.

Today was a big day. Today she would get her first glimpse of the people who stood between her and her rightful place in the Chesterfield's kitchen.

Luck.

The only kind Finn Westbrook had experienced since his divorce two years earlier was the bad variety. In spades. Now here he was, running late for the opportunity of a lifetime, and he'd lost his ride in a stupid game of chance. Still, as he watched the cab pull away with the pretty young woman tucked inside, he couldn't complain.

She wasn't the sort of female who would have turned most men's heads, especially at a mere glance. Her looks were too understated for that: small, freckle-dusted nose; arched brows that all but disappeared beneath a fringe of bangs; lips that were not quite as full as was the current fashion; wide-set green eyes that, up close, revealed flecks of gold.

But the moment their hands touched, she'd had Finn's

attention trussed up like a holiday turkey. In that moment, he'd experienced something he hadn't felt for a woman in a very long time: attraction. The real, punch-in-the-gut kind that knocked the wind out of a guy for a split second before his breathing resumed in a white-hot rush.

Damn, if it didn't feel good. He'd been dead inside for so long. And that kiss? Heat was still licking through his veins, threatening to consume him. He settled his hands on his hips and shook his head in amazement.

Fate, bitch that she was, chose that moment to offer a swift kick where it counted. The rain that had held off during their game of Rock, Paper, Scissors gushed from the sky like water sprayed from the business end of a fire hose. Still, Finn could only smile. Maybe he should be grateful for a dousing of cold water.

CHAPTER TWO

Peel and chop

BY THE TIME Lara reached her destination, she'd managed to push thoughts of the sexy man to the back burner. But those nerves had her feeling as if she'd eaten bad shellfish. She paid the cabbie and, holding her purse over her head, made a dash for the building, dodging raindrops and umbrella-wielding pedestrians as she went.

At the reception desk in the lobby, she checked in, donned a visitor's badge that bore the name Lara Smith and headed for the nearest elevator with a sigh of relief. She'd cleared the first hurdle. She'd half expected someone to recognize her, new bangs notwithstanding, and call her out on the alias.

On the fifteenth floor, the waiting room for Sylvan Studios was crowded with people. The best of the best in the industry sat in the tastefully upholstered chairs. They were an eclectic-looking bunch, but that was to be expected. Chefs came in all varieties, from the artsy and avant-garde to the down-home and downright dowdy. She knew better than to discount any of them based on appearance alone. All of them had won their preliminary round and were after the same thing as Lara: a job.

Not just any job, but one that would have been hers if she hadn't taken her rebellion to the extreme. Leave it to

her father to rub salt in the wound by publicly proclaiming
the need for a "successor," and then agreeing to let Cuisine
Cable Network fill the head-chef position at his restaurant
via its highly rated *Executive Chef Challenge* show. By
the time the last of the weekly installments aired in the
fall, Lara or one of eleven other über-qualified chefs from
around the country would be deciding the Chesterfield's
dinner specials.

Lara had entered the competition without her father's
knowledge. Indeed, no one at the network knew about her
ties to Clifton and the Chesterfield. She could only count
on anonymity because the program was taped in advance.
If it aired live, she would have been found out right away.
If she made it to the final round, which her father would
judge personally, she would be forced to come clean. Between now and then, however, she had to do some of the
best and most creative cooking of her life.

She scanned the faces of the six men and four women
in the waiting room. Add her and that made eleven. She
frowned. Someone was missing.

She was still standing just inside the door, surreptitiously
checking email on her cell phone, when she heard it open.
Contestant number twelve had arrived. She turned, ready
to size up the competition, and came face-to-face with...

"Paper," she murmured in surprise and resisted the urge
to touch her lips.

The gray eyes regarding her widened fractionally before
his mouth softened with a grin.

"Actually, I go by Finn. Finn Westbrook." He peeled
off his drenched jacket and hung it on the coatrack just to
Lara's left. "Enjoy your ride?"

"I did. Thank you." Even though the answer seemed
obvious, she inquired, "Did you have to wait long for another taxi?"

"I gave up on waiting there. I hauled ass for three blocks before I was able to flag one down at Columbus Circle."

A drop of water spilled down his temple. Lara resisted the temptation to wipe it away. Instead, she reached into her purse and handed him a plastic-wrapped package of tissues.

"Thanks."

"Least I can do. I didn't realize we both were headed to the same place or we could have shared the taxi."

He pulled out a couple of the tissues, gave her back the packet and blotted his temple before rubbing them over his head. His short hair looked both messy and perfect afterward.

"So, you're a chef," he said.

"That's right." And although she was pretty sure she knew the answer, she said, "You?"

"One of the best." The smile that accompanied the boast was charming enough to keep his words from sounding too cocky.

"I'm pretty sure everyone in this room can make the same claim," she replied drily.

His smile widened as he balled up the tissues and, after little more than a cursory glance, tossed them in the direction of a wastebasket that was tucked in the corner. The soggy wad made it in. Of course. More points for him…if she were keeping score.

"I guess this means we're adversaries," he said.

Indeed. They both were after the same thing. The very thing for which he'd sought out a good-luck kiss. *Keep your eyes on the prize, Lara*, she silently admonished, since she was finding keeping her eyes on Finn a far-too-pleasing diversion.

"I guess it does."

His gaze lowered to her mouth, lingered for a couple of heartbeats. "That's too bad."

Before Lara could think of a fitting response, a man

stepped out from one of the offices. He was in his late thirties, suit-clad and bespectacled with a receding hairline. But what made him seem older and headmasterish was the way he clapped his hands together to gain their attention.

She recognized him from the preliminary round that she'd won a couple of weeks earlier. His name was Tristan Wembley, and he worked for the network in some sort of production capacity. She couldn't remember his official title, but he'd made it clear in their previous dealings that if Lara had any questions or concerns, she was to contact him first.

"Welcome, everyone, to Sylvan Studios, the home of the Cuisine Cable Network and its highest-rated program, *Executive Chef Challenge*, which, as you know, is featuring the famed Chesterfield restaurant this season.

"Congratulations on making it this far in the competition. It's a testament to your skill as chefs that you are standing here right now. One hundred and eighty-two other hopefuls didn't make the cut.

"Today, you will get your first look at the kitchen studio. Tomorrow and Friday, we will spend the day taping promo spots that will be televised and also air on our website. Filming of the first round starts Monday morning. You are to report to the studio no later than 7:00 a.m. Plan on spending at least ten hours here."

Someone gasped. "Ten hours!"

"It may be closer to twelve," Tristan replied, unfazed.

Even though the segments would air weekly on the network, the chefs would be competing three days a week for nearly four weeks. She was in for some long days.

Tristan's upbeat tone took an ominous turn when he said, "Take a good look around, chefs, because by this time next week, one of you already will have been sent packing and another one will be on his or her way out the door."

Lara scanned the waiting room's occupants, wondering whom it would be. No way was she leaving after the first round or the second. When she got to Finn, he snorted softly and leaned over to whisper, "Don't look at me. I'm not going anywhere. I'm in it for the duration."

Under other circumstances, she might have welcomed those words from a gorgeous man whose mouth should be registered as a lethal weapon. In this case…

A tremor swept up her spine. "God, I hope not."

The corners of Finn's mouth turned down even as his brows shot up. His tone held a slight edge when he replied, "At least you're honest."

If he only knew…

Tristan clapped his hands together again.

"Okay, chefs, if you'll follow me, we can get started."

Finn fell in step beside Lara.

"I guess you regret that kiss for luck now," he said conversationally.

She glanced around, thankful that none of the other chefs appeared to have overheard them. Lip-locks with strangers for good luck wasn't exactly a topic she wanted broadcasted.

"Probably as much as you're regretting letting me have that cab," she replied, keeping her voice so low that he leaned closer to hear her. She swore she could feel the heat wafting from his hot, moist skin.

"You won the cab." Broad shoulders lifted and his gaze lowered to her lips again. "As for anything else, I'm not beating myself up over it. It was…nice."

"Nice?" She replied too quickly to edit the incredulity from her tone.

"You have a better adjective for it?" His tone held a dare. She shook her head and he went on.

"It's a little inconvenient, though."

"I don't know what you mean," she said innocently.

He smiled, looking as satisfied as Lara had felt after that amazing kiss. "I think you do."

Oh, yeah. She did, all right.

He went on. "I want you to know in advance that I'm sorry."

"For?"

"Taking you down."

The grin that stole over his face now was worthy of a plundering pirate.

"Damn, you're arrogant." But she said it without any heat. In fact, she couldn't hold back her own smile.

Ahead of them, Tristan was saying, "Each of you has been randomly assigned a workstation. All of the stations are identical with identical supplies. Today, you will have one hour—no more, no less—to acquaint yourself with the space and set it up as you see fit.

"If something is missing or an appliance doesn't work properly, it's your responsibility to tell one of the staff before you leave today. Once filming starts on Monday, no adjustments will be made. None," he stated firmly with a steely glance around. "You will just have to make do."

Tristan had walked while he talked. The group now stood outside the studio. Over the double doors a red light was encased in a metal cage. It was off now, indicating that no taping was going on. Soon enough the set would be hot and filming would be under way.

As a food stylist, Lara had spent a great deal of time under bright lights and around cameras. She'd considered that good training for this competition. She'd even figured it might give her a leg up on her opponents—until Tristan pushed open the doors and they all filed inside.

The overhead lights glared off the appliances as well as the stainless-steel-topped prep stations.

Someone yelled, "Sweet!"

And she heard a few oaths, some uttered in awe, others laced with foreboding. Hers fell into the latter category.

"It looks different on television," Finn said.

It certainly did. On TV it seemed smaller, almost intimate. It looked like a real restaurant kitchen rather than a massive set riddled with cables and camera equipment.

Ovens and prep stations lined two of the walls. The third wall boasted a pantry, an impressively stocked wine rack and a double-door refrigerator, as well as an ice-cream machine, blast chiller, anti-griddle and other specialized appliances.

The setup allowed for the contestants as well as the camera operators to move around freely. And, of course, come Monday, the show's on-air host, Garrett St. John, would be there as well, roaming the set while he narrated the competitors' actions and performed spontaneous on-air interviews as they worked.

On-air interviews.

Bile threatened to creep up the back of her throat at the thought. She'd scored a C-minus in public speaking in high school. Too much lip-smacking and too many *ums*, according to her teacher. Oh, and she talked too fast and failed to make enough eye contact with the audience.

"If anyone suffers stage fright, I suggest you get over it now," Tristan said. "In addition to the twelve of you, this set will be crowded with several dozen other people next week. A number of them will be operating cameras trained not only on what you are making, but on your faces. You may have as many as a dozen focused on you at any given time. Every grin, every grimace, every little dot of perspiration on your forehead will be recorded."

"Gee, that makes me feel better," Lara murmured thickly.

Next to her, Finn grunted out what passed for a laugh.

Tristan was saying, "When the show airs, the fans will be rooting for their favorites. We want to give them as much of you as possible. That's why a lot of what doesn't make it into each week's televised episode will wind up on the show's website."

Tristan's cell rang. He glanced at the display.

"Sorry. I need to take this. And while I do, I need for all of you to wait here. No searching for your workstations until I return," he added before walking out in the hallway to talk on his phone.

"Nervous?" Finn asked.

Heck, yeah, she was nervous. But she shook her head and tried to look unconcerned.

Her denial was met with one raised eyebrow. "And I thought you were honest," he chided softly.

"Okay, maybe I'm a little nervous," she allowed. "Not about cooking for the judges or having to do it while facing down a clock, but—"

"Liar."

She ignored him and continued. "But about the entertainment component. I'm a chef, not an actor." She gestured around her. "I think we're all nervous about working in front of the cameras."

"Speak for yourself."

"Are you telling me you're not the least bit anxious?"

"I can't afford to be if I want to win. And I want to win."

"Wanting isn't the same as doing."

The smile her word elicited was illicit. He leaned closer, and his tone was matter-of-fact when he clarified, "I'm going to win."

Another time she might have found such self-assuredness sexy, especially when paired with smoky eyes and a devilish grin. Since it ran counter to her own plans, however, she told him, "In your dreams, Paper."

Finn chuckled. "I was right about figuring you for a rock. But the only thing I'm dreaming about right now—" His gaze flicked to her lips and he hesitated before clarifying,

"The only thing I can *afford* to dream about is being the last chef standing in this kitchen."

"That makes two of us."

"Try a dozen of us," scoffed the young man standing to Lara's right.

She'd forgotten about him—she'd forgotten about *all* of them—as she and Finn had engaged in a quiet battle of words that carried an undertone of flirting.

Kirby Something-or-other. From where she stood, she wasn't able to make out the last name on his badge. She pegged him to be in his early twenties. His shaggy hair stuck out at odd angles and gave the overall appearance of having been hacked off with a meat cleaver.

"That doesn't mean we can't all be friendly, y'all." The speaker this time was a middle-aged blonde whose waist was as thick as her Southern accent. Her badge read *Flo Gimball*.

"That's right. We can be friendly. Course, it won't change anything. I'm going to win," boasted a gravelly-voiced man who sported a shaved head, gauged ears and a five-inch-long goatee.

Thanks to two full sleeves of tattoos, he would have looked right at home in a biker bar. Rebel that he was, he wasn't wearing the name tag he'd received from the security desk in the lobby, but the Gothic lettering on the side of his neck spelled out *Ryder*. Lara assumed it was his name—whether first, last or otherwise, she couldn't be sure.

"Right," she muttered half under her breath.

Sorry, but she couldn't see Ryder in her father's kitchen. For starters, Clifton wasn't a fan of body art, which was probably why she had gotten a yin-yang symbol the size of a half-dollar inked on her lower back as soon as she'd turned eighteen. Her dad had been livid when he found out. She'd been smug and secretly pleased to have gotten his attention. Now, every time she wore a bathing suit, she just felt stupid.

"You got something to say?" Ryder asked in a voice as gritty as cornmeal.

The guy easily stood six-six and carried his fillet knife in a sheath attached to his belt. Fish and prime cuts of meat probably weren't the only things he used it on. Lara gulped, a purely reflexive action that she regretted immediately when the huge man grinned as if he could smell her fear.

"Down, boy." Finn surprised her by stepping between them. "Pick on someone your own size."

Ryder's laughter chewed through the silence that followed Finn's valiant admonition like the rusty blade of a chain saw.

"I musta missed the memo that said we're competing in pairs. What, pretty boy? Are you gonna be her sous-chef?" Ryder taunted.

The barb earned snickers from some of the other competitors.

Lara appreciated Finn's gesture, but she couldn't afford to be perceived as weak. Stepping around him, she told Ryder, "Actually, I do have something to say, but I'll let my food do the talking on Monday."

For that matter, she hoped that whatever she prepared in the allotted time would speak volumes to the trio of judges, which would include a different celebrity chef each week.

"Should be pretty quiet, then," said a statuesque brunette whose name badge read *Angel Horvath*.

Her overinflated lips curved into a smile that was too menacing to be perceived as friendly, and Lara was left with the impression that it wouldn't be smart to turn her back on the woman—or any of her fellow competitors, for that matter.

That included Finn, their kiss in the cab and his recent act of gallantry notwithstanding. They all had the same objective: winning. As Finn already had pointed out, that made them adversaries.

Tristan had returned for part of the exchange. He clapped his hands together again in a gesture that Lara was already starting to find annoying.

"Hey, chefs. I have no problem with trash talk. In fact, undermining another contestant's confidence can be a good strategy. But save it for the cameras, please. We have too much to do over the next couple of days to waste time on your egos."

Lara cast a sideways glance at Finn. The easygoing smile he'd sported was gone, replaced by an expression more in keeping with the intensity she'd spied earlier in his gaze. His game face, she thought, and experienced a flicker of disappointment that they hadn't met under other circumstances.

CHAPTER THREE

Mix well

THE COMPETITORS HAD one hour, not a minute more, to familiarize themselves with their surroundings. Finn had to restrain himself to a brisk walk when Tristan finally released them to go find their workstations. He wanted to run like a couple of the other chefs were doing, but he knew better. Haste in a kitchen was often met with disaster. So he moved quickly, but safely as he searched for his name on the white placards affixed to the stainless-steel vent hoods.

Finn had spent his entire adult life in and around professional kitchens—some of them better equipped and better run than others. For a while, he'd presided over his own in a restaurant dubbed Rascal's, which he'd owned with his wife and best friend. Ex-wife now. And former best friend.

He was at home amid pots, pans and appliances, but he wasn't exactly in his element here.

Finn hadn't admitted it before, but he shared Lara's trepidation about cooking in front of a slew of cameras for a television audience that ultimately would not taste his creations. He had no problem preparing his signature dishes in a crowded restaurant kitchen where well-ordered chaos reigned, but this was different. So much in the Cuisine Cable Network's kitchen was unknown, unaccounted for and just plain beyond his control.

It came down to a hand of cards. Literally. At the start of each competition the host would deal three oversize cards. One specified the amount of time the chefs had to cook. Another gave the course they had to prepare—appetizer, entrée or dessert. The final card revealed the identity of the celebrity judge.

And then there was the plainspoken and pretty Lara Smith.

If the first blow of attraction had landed like a sucker punch, the second, when he'd stumbled upon her in the waiting room, had delivered the knockout.

Wouldn't it just figure that the first woman to arouse his interest—and then some—since Sheryl had buried a knife in his back would be one he was competing against for the chance of a lifetime?

Priorities, Westbrook, priorities, he silently admonished.

Sex and his social life rated lower on the list than getting back what he'd lost. And thanks to Sheryl and Cole, he'd lost everything.

Of course, all of the chefs here were determined to win. But it was different for Finn. For him, it went deeper than bragging rights and securing a coveted position with a paycheck to match. Being crowned the Chesterfield's executive chef wouldn't be a stop as much as a stepping-stone. He needed it to launch his comeback.

Nothing and no one would stand in his way.

He found his station and smothered a bemused laugh. So much for putting distance between himself and Lara Smith. They would be working side by side.

At the moment, however, it wasn't her side that had Finn's attention. She was bent at the waist, inspecting the oven. It was all he could do to hold back a groan at his first unrestricted view of her butt. Overall, she was too slender to be considered voluptuous, but her rear had a definite curve that filled out her fitted pants nicely. If she liked to sample her cooking, as chefs were wont to do, she worked off the extra calories later. When his libido started to fantasize about exactly how, he swallowed hard and reeled it in.

She glanced over as she straightened, and smiled.

"We meet again," he said in a lame attempt to cover his embarrassment over being caught ogling her butt.

The bright lights teased streaks of copper from her otherwise auburn hair, and idly he wondered if it was as soft to the touch as it appeared.

"That reminds me. I never properly introduced myself." She rubbed the palm of her right hand on the thigh of her pants before holding it out. "I'm—"

"No need." A handshake? Really? They'd already kissed. "Besides, I know who you are."

"Y-you know?" Her eyes rounded at that and her face paled to the point he thought she might pass out.

It was a curious reaction. She didn't only sound surprised but, well, guilty.

"You're wearing a badge with your name on it," he pointed out.

"I… A badge. Right. I'm wearing a badge." She laughed awkwardly as she patted the rectangular sticker affixed to a chest that, in his estimation, was neither too large nor too small, but just the right size. She motioned to the prep table that they would be sharing. "It looks like we're going to be working together."

The idea, like the woman, was way too appealing for his peace of mind, so he clarified, "We won't be working together, Lara. We'll be competing against each other."

"Adversaries," she said, parroting what he had said earlier.

"Yep. And as I already told you, I intend to win."

She notched up her chin, not appearing to be cowed in the least by his bravado.

He found her arrogance a surprising turn-on when she

replied in a haughty voice, "You keep telling yourself that, Paper. You just keep telling yourself that."

Smooth.

Lara patted the badge even as she wanted to give her forehead a slap. She supposed the fact that she was so lousy at lying was a testament to how rarely she did it. Deceit did not come naturally to her. No, that would be her mother.

Even with her father—*especially* with him—Lara had always been truthful. Blunt and tactless, yes, but truthful all the same.

At least Finn was no longer staring at her as if she'd grown a second head. In fact, he wasn't looking at her at all. He was going about his business, as should she, since they had only an hour in the kitchen studio.

Satisfied that the oven and stove-top burners worked, Lara turned her attention to the prep table. While all of the contestants had their own ovens, the tables, which ran parallel to them, were ten feet long and intended to accommodate two chefs. All of her preparations, including plating the finished product, would take place on that single length of stainless-steel real estate, and she was going to have to share it with the handsome man who had her mind wandering to other uses for a handy horizontal surface.

"Something wrong?" He stopped what he was doing and looked over at her.

Lara felt a flush creep over her cheeks, one of the curses of having a redhead's fair skin.

"No. Nothing's…wrong." She forced her gaze from him to the prep top, where a couple of containers filled with spatulas, slotted spoons and the like, and some bottles of oil were all that delineated one chef's side from the other. "It's just not a lot of space for two people."

"Worried I'll take advantage of you?"

She felt her face flame anew as a couple of more inappropriate thoughts threatened to storm the gates of propriety. Worried? More like wishing.

"I just hope you're not one of those chefs who like to spread out."

"I'll keep all of my stuff on my side if you'll do the same." To illustrate his point, Finn moved a bottle of extra virgin olive oil to his section.

"Actually, I think we're supposed to share the oil."

He glanced at the trio of bottles, which were filled with different varieties, some of which were intended for cooking, others for adding flavor afterward.

"Ah. So I see." He moved the bottle back to the dividing line. "Are we good?"

"That depends." She canted her leg out to one side and settled a hand on her hip. She was only half kidding when she said, "When you're cooking, are you neat? Some chefs aren't and it's a pet peeve of mine."

Indeed, it was one of the rare points on which Lara and her father actually saw eye to eye.

"As a pin. What about you?"

"A place for everything and everything in its place."

"Then I'd say the two of us will get along fine."

"Yes, we're…" Her gaze homed in on his mouth as she recalled their kiss. "We're very…"

Finn's smirk told her he knew exactly where her mind had wandered.

"*Compatible?* Is that the word you're looking for?"

Oh, she had a feeling they would be that and then some.

She looked away and blurted out the first thing she could think of. "The knives aren't bad."

Five of the most essential blades clung to magnetic strips that were mounted on the wall behind each contestant's stove. Even at a glance, she could gauge the quality. The network had spared no expense.

"Will you be using them?" he asked.

"Please." She snorted at that. More so than any other utensil in a chef's kitchen, knives were personal, their weight and balance suited to the user. As such, they were the one item the contestants were allowed to bring with them from home. "Are you kidding?"

He shrugged. "Just trying to get a feel for what kind of chef you are."

She was the kind who deserved to be heading up the Chesterfield's kitchen, a job she was going to do her damnedest to earn.

Tristan, apparently having overheard their conversation, said, "Remember, chefs. You're limited to seven." He'd been making the rounds in the studio, hands clasped behind his back, his expression reminiscent of a warden's. "Are you finding everything to be in working order at your stations?"

"So far so good," Finn said.

She nodded in agreement.

Once Tristan had moved on, Finn said, "I wonder if Ryder will show up next week wearing *all* of his knives on his belt. The guy's a trip."

The visual nearly had her smiling.

"I was going to say *scary*. Thanks for earlier, by the way."

She might not have needed Finn's interference, but she'd appreciated the gesture.

"He was just trying to psych you out."

Mind games.

For a sobering second she wondered if Finn was playing one now, being nice, friendly, lulling her into complacency with words that were every bit as enticing as his good looks. She didn't want to think so, but as Tristan had mentioned earlier, a chef could use trickery and deceit as part of his or her overall strategy.

Underhandedness made for good television. Still, Lara couldn't see her father condoning such behavior in the person tapped to run his kitchen. Of course, Clifton wouldn't have much of a choice—at least not for one year. She'd read the fine print in the rules. The winner was ensured employment as the head chef for that long, although he or she could be fired for cause before then.

"What made you sign on for this?" Finn asked.

Lara opted for the most obvious answer, which also saved her from having to lie. She felt like enough of a fraud already. "I want the job. You?"

"The same." He said it quickly, a little *too* quickly.

They eyed one another.

"It's a great opportunity. The chance of a lifetime." She smiled.

"It's also a lot of hoops to jump through to run your own kitchen."

"It's not just *any* kitchen, though. It's the Chesterfield. Two American presidents have eaten there, as well as an assortment of state and federal lawmakers. On any given night you can find a Tony-Award-winning actor or Hollywood A-lister seated in the dining room raving about the roasted duck or—"

She broke off, becoming aware that she sounded just like her father used to when Lara or her mother had dared to complain about the amount of time he spent there.

Meanwhile, Finn didn't appear overly awed, even when he leaned closer and added, "You forgot its Michelin rating. Three stars."

Okay, now she was confused. "You're not impressed?"

"Oh, I'm impressed, all right. I wouldn't be here otherwise." He was holding one of the knives, and he used it to make a sweeping motion around the studio. "Even so, I'd bet you the title that more than a few of the chefs here have a reason beyond the Chesterfield's prestige for signing up for this show."

Lara glanced around, considering. Perhaps Finn was

right. He certainly was right about her. She had something
to prove. To her father. To herself. And, okay, maybe she
could perform a little bit of penance in the process.

He was saying, "It's those reasons you have to worry
about."

Intrigued, she asked, "What do you mean?"

"That's where passion comes from."

Finn returned the knife to the magnetic strip, offered
the same smile that he'd given her after he'd surrendered
the cab and asked for that kiss. The effect was every bit as
mesmerizing. Lara's skin felt as if it had been splattered
with hot grease.

With her gaze on his mouth, she almost corrected him.
It wasn't passion's only origin.

They didn't talk for the next several minutes as they ac-
quainted themselves not only with their immediate stations but also the set's overall configuration. Indeed, the
kitchen was unnaturally quiet. All of the chefs were alert
and on edge.

The pantry consisted of several freestanding, metal-
framed shelving units. An assortment of bins and containers, contents clearly labeled in bold lettering, filled them.

"So, that's a red onion," the quirky-haired Kirby said.

Lara, Finn and several of the other chefs laughed.

Tristan adjusted his glasses and allowed a moment for
their mirth before saying, "Obviously, the labels are intended for viewers at home. Although in the heat of battle,
some of you also might find yourselves grateful for them."

"I notice that several of these are empty, Tristan." Flo
pointed to a bin marked *Bell Peppers*.

"Not to worry. They'll be full on Monday with fresh
produce."

"How fresh?" Lara wanted to know. "And where does
the show do its shopping?"

"You're the food stylist, right?" Tristan asked.

Other than her pseudonym, Lara had tried to be as truthful as possible on her application to the show. So, in addition to her education and professional background, she'd jotted down her current job title.

Ryder snickered, apparently sharing her father's derogatory opinion of her profession.

She squared her shoulders. "That's my current job, yes. And, as a food stylist, I know that the fresher the ingredients, the better-looking the finished product. The same, obviously, goes for taste. There is a huge difference between the flavor of a tomato allowed to ripen on the vine before it's picked and shipped to a nearby market, and a hydroponic pretender trucked to a grocery store half a dozen states away. I don't want that difference to cost me with the judges."

"She makes a good point," Finn said while several of the other chefs nodded. "I'll be damned if I want to go home because some college intern didn't know how to pick out decent broccoli rabe."

Lara appreciated his solidarity.

"I can assure you, everything used on this show is carefully selected. We shop the same sources as high-end restaurants do and that includes the Chesterfield. Sometimes we shop directly from local growers. The same goes for our seafood, meat and poultry. Buyers for the show are at the seaport before dawn on weekdays picking out the best catches. Quality will not be an issue." He eyed Finn before adding drily, "At least not the quality of the ingredients."

Rather than being offended, Finn merely smiled. "Touché."

It was interesting. The man could be intense, but apparently that didn't prevent him from also having a sense of humor or poking fun at himself. Lara found it an appealing trait. God knew that neither her father nor her ex-husband had been able to laugh at themselves.

"One thing to keep in mind, chefs." Tristan held up a finger as he revealed the troubling caveat. "Although the pantry items will be restocked after every round of competition, once they are gone during a round, they're gone."

"First come, first served. Sounds good to me. Get used to seeing me at the front of the line," Ryder said to no one in particular as he folded a pair of tattooed arms over his massive chest.

Lara offered up a silent prayer that he would be the first in line for elimination, as well. Less than an hour in his presence and his unflagging superiority had grown tiresome. She really didn't want to have to put up with it for the show's duration.

"This is a competition intended to test your skills, Mr. Surkovski." Ryder's last name, Lara assumed as Tristan continued, "Sometimes even the best kitchens run out of an item and have to make adjustments on the fly. You've got to use your head. In other words, brain trumps brawn here. You'll have to rely on what can be found between your earrings."

Where Finn had taken Tristan's teasing barbs in stride, Ryder's skin flushed a deep scarlet and his eyes narrowed to dangerous slits. Lara figured it was only Tristan's position with the network that saved him from a scathing comeback. Or worse.

"The first kitchen I worked in ran out of hot dogs. It was a disaster since it was at the ballpark," Finn quipped to no one in particular.

Lara got the feeling Finn had only said it to lighten the mood. Sure enough, Tristan and the other chefs laughed. All except for Ryder. He was stone-faced.

"You're making an enemy," Lara whispered as they followed Tristan to another area of the set.

"You mean Ryder?" Finn shrugged, apparently unconcerned. "It's not like I'm here to make friends."

Adversaries. The word rang in her head. Right.

They could be friendly, but they were competitors, each with an agenda that ran counter to the others'. Under such circumstances, true friendship or relationships of any kind weren't likely.

So it came as a surprise when, after they finished with everything for the day, Finn turned to Lara as they headed outside and said, "Hey, do you want to go for a cup of coffee or something?"

God help her, but it was the *or something* that had her attention.

CHAPTER FOUR

Add a dash of spice

"I THOUGHT YOU told me you weren't here to make friends, Finn," Lara said, raising one eyebrow.

"I'm not."

"But you're willing to make an exception in my case?"

Was he?

One side of her mouth rose in a smile that had a decidedly unsettling effect on his heart rate. No, Finn wasn't after friendship. But he couldn't deny his interest in Lara Smith. It had been there since the get-go.

"Well, if you looked like Ryder, I wouldn't be offering," he replied truthfully.

"And if I looked like Angel?"

"What do you mean by that?" he asked.

"Smoky eyes and Angelina Jolie lips?" Lara pouted and batted her eyelashes for effect. "Not to mention a pair of legs that start at the chin."

"There's nothing wrong with your legs." Or any other part of her anatomy, from what Finn could tell. And, yeah, he'd been looking. "Besides, she's not my taste. Too…obvious." His gaze lowered briefly to Lara's mouth and more naturally proportioned lips before flicking away to gaze up at the busy street. "I prefer subtlety, complexity."

"Are you talking about women or are you talking about food?"

"Both, I guess." He laughed.

She nodded, as if processing that. Then, "I'm still not clear on why you want to have coffee with me."

Why indeed? He wasn't quite clear on that himself. So, what he went with was "Ever hear the saying, 'Keep your friends close and your enemies closer'?"

"Gee, you know how to make a girl feel special."

He laughed at her deadpan delivery. He'd always found a good sense of humor attractive in a woman.

"Actually, I've got a job in this neighborhood in a couple of hours. It doesn't make sense to go home, and I don't feel like sitting alone while I kill time."

"Kill time," she repeated. He nearly winced. Had he really just said that? "That's a lukewarm invitation, you know. You need to work on your people skills, Paper."

She had a point. He was a little rusty when it came to flirting with women. The ink on his divorce decree might have been dry for a couple of years, but Finn hadn't gone out much. He'd been too busy. And, yeah, too bitter.

He wasn't feeling bitter now. Oh, no. The emotions pinging around in his head were a lot more palatable than that.

"Is that no?"

"I should go home," she told him. "I mean, I have laundry to do."

"Laundry?" He placed a hand over his heart. "You're turning me down to go home and throw in a load of dirty clothes?"

A smile lurked on her lips when Lara added, "Well, my refrigerator needs to be cleaned out, too."

"Yeah. *That* makes me feel better. What? No game of Candy Crush calling your name?"

"How did you know?" Her full-on grin had his heart

doing a funny *thu-thunk*. "But I can multitask and do that while I'm waiting for my clothes to dry."

"Who needs to work on people skills now?" he asked sardonically.

"Fine." Her grin made a mockery of the sigh that followed. "I'll have a cup of coffee with you."

Finn nodded, more pleased than he wanted to be that she'd accepted his invitation.

"I know a coffee shop not far from here that makes excellent biscotti."

"You're not talking about Isadora's, are you?"

"That's the one." He blinked in surprise. "You know it?"

"Best biscotti in all of Manhattan. And the coffee is pretty good, too."

Together, they headed off in the direction of the café. The rain had stopped. In fact, little evidence of the earlier downpour remained except for errant puddles in places where the sidewalk dipped. He watched Lara widen her stride to step over one. Her legs weren't as long as the aforementioned Angel's, but they were slender, which gave them the illusion of length. And he'd bet they were toned, too, based both on the way her pants fit and the lithe grace with which she moved.

Although she was petite, she hadn't worn dangerously high heels to compensate. Her footwear choice on this day was a sensible pair of flats whose only bow to femininity was a row of flirty ruffles that crossed the toe. They were a practical choice for the kitchen, although he'd noticed that Amazon-sized Angel had gone with spikes and even down-home Flo had opted for a wedged heel that added a couple of inches to her otherwise average height.

Lara was saying, "I'm at Isadora's at least twice a week, although I limit my biscotto intake to one piece once a week."

Disciplined, he thought. But what surprised him was

the fact they hadn't met before now given their affinity for both the hard Italian cookie and the place.

"I'm there most weekday mornings. I bring my laptop, clear my email, that sort of thing. I can't believe I've never run into you."

"I know. What time do you arrive? I usually show up around seven, and then I'm in and out pretty fast. I get my order to go."

"Seven?" Finn whistled through his teeth. "That explains it. I'm still in bed at seven. In fact, I rarely throw back the covers before nine."

She blinked as if trying to clear away an inappropriate visual. Or maybe his ego just wanted to believe that was the case.

"Night owl?" she asked.

"I didn't used to be, but…" He shrugged. "I work as a private chef now, so I'm a night owl if my client is, and lately, she is."

"She?" Lara's eyebrows rose.

"I signed a confidentiality clause, so that's about all I'm allowed to say."

"Ah. Someone famous, then. Got it." She nodded before asking, "Do you have a lot of freedom to plan the menu or does your client tell you what she wants and how she wants it?"

Finn couldn't stop his laugher. He didn't try, even when a blush stained Lara's cheeks.

"You make me sound like a gigolo," he responded once he'd managed to catch his breath. "I know food can be a sensual experience, but…"

"Sorry. I—"

He shook his head and waved off the apology. Then Lara did it again, put her foot right back in that very appealing mouth of hers.

"It must pay pretty well. Otherwise, why would you…?

I mean, obviously, you'd rather run a restaurant kitchen." She squinted through one eye. "That came out wrong."

"That's all right." Hell, sometimes Finn felt as if he'd sold out, but a guy had to make a living and at least he was still able to do so with his cooking. "To answer your first poorly phrased question—" He laughed again. "I plan the menus, but sometimes she makes a request. And she likes to have dinner parties, so…"

"Late nights."

"Exactly. Tonight included. I'll be lucky to plant my face in my pillow by three."

"It's Wednesday."

"Yeah. Welcome to the life of the idle rich."

Isadora's was just ahead on the other side of the street. Finn swore he could already smell the coffee on the stale afternoon breeze. They stopped at the curb. While they waited for the light to change, he asked, "What kind of coffee do you drink?" He tipped his head to one side. "You're not one of those half-caf-with-skim-milk women, are you?"

"And if I say yes?"

"I'd have to turn you on to the beauty of a plain old cup of freshly brewed French roast."

Her brows notched up.

Now who was guilty of poor phrasing? Finn thought. But she didn't call him on it.

Instead, she agreed, "Simplicity is underrated."

"Yep. Everyone wants to complicate things, thinking that somehow makes the end result better."

Finn wasn't only talking about coffee now, but the direction his kitchen—and he still considered Rascal's kitchen his—had gone under Sheryl's and Cole's leadership. Rascal's, named for the classic *Our Gang* reruns he'd watched as a kid, had featured traditional food with fun, funky twists. These days the menu was more classical than classic, heavy with French influences that ran counter to the eclectic decor and irreverent name.

"Personally, I like Colombian and I look for organic beans harvested and sold under Fair Trade. Does that make me high maintenance or too trendy?" she wanted to know.

"Even if it did, at least it would be for a good cause."

"So, it's okay to be picky or demanding if you're doing it for a good cause?"

Finn laughed. "Something like that."

They arrived at the shop and he held open the door for her. At this hour of the day, the place wasn't very busy. Most people already had reached their daily caffeine quota. A few professional types in business suits stood in line at the take-out window. In the dining room, trendily dressed girls whom he guessed to be high school age sat laughing at one table. Two other tables were taken by preoccupied twentysomethings tapping away on their laptop keyboards.

"Counter or table?" she asked.

"Your choice."

Lara turned and started toward a table that was wedged against the window. It was the one he often sat at so he could watch the foot traffic file past. As he sat down, he could hear the slight buzzing of the neon Open sign overhead. A waitress was over almost immediately to take their orders.

Lara went with Colombian. He went with French roast. They both took their coffee black. Another reason to like her, he decided. Food required seasoning. But a good cup of coffee didn't need to be doctored up with cream, whether flavored or plain. Nor did it need sweetener of any sort. Especially if one was going to be dunking cookies in it.

"I'll have the macadamia-nut-and-dried-cranberry biscotto," she told the waitress.

"Make that two." It was what he always ordered, as well.

After the waitress left, Lara quipped, "We made her job easy."

"We can always send the biscotti back and complain about the coffee to test her patience and make her earn the tip we leave."

"I'm sure she's already waited on more than a couple people like that today. I've worked in enough kitchens to know that some people make special requests or send back food just to be a pain in the rear."

He cocked his head to one side and studied her. "I thought you were a food stylist."

Lara pointed at his mouth. "Did you know that your lip curled when you said that?"

"It did not."

She nodded. "Afraid so."

"Okay, maybe a little. It just seems like a poor use of your talent." And obviously she had talent or she wouldn't have made it on to the show.

Tone dry as dust, she replied, "Says the man who pimps out his cooking to the highest bidder. What's the story behind that?"

"We're talking about you right now. We'll get to my story later." He wasn't sure what he would share with her. But right now he wanted to know more about her, so he asked, "Do you enjoy styling other people's food?"

"I'm very good at it."

"But that's not what I asked."

The waitress returned with their coffees and biscotti. Lara picked up one of the hard Italian cookies and dunked it into her cup. Stalling?

Finn prompted, "Well?"

"Sure. I enjoy it. I wouldn't do it otherwise. Appearances are important."

"Appearances can be deceiving," he shot back.

That was true both in the case of a roasted turkey that

had been brushed with oil to make it look moist and a fresh-faced woman with secrets brimming in her eyes.

"Yes. And no. I'm willing to go out on a limb and bet that Ryder does not sing in a church choir."

But did Ryder have something to hide? Finn didn't think so. He was an in-your-face kind of guy. Lara Smith? The way she sometimes acted, Finn wondered.

"All right, I'll come clean," she said only to end with, "I like cooking more."

Not exactly a revelation, but it was a start.

"Where did you go to culinary school?"

She named off the very institution that he had attended, although he'd graduated a few years ahead of her. When she mentioned training abroad under a couple of world-renowned chefs, Finn was duly impressed and whistled through his teeth.

"How did you manage that? As far as I know, neither of those guys hires anything but seasoned veterans to work in their kitchens. Even their prep chefs and line cooks have been around the block a time or two."

Yet Lara had scored an internship.

"My father's doing."

"Your father?"

Rather than answer right away, she bit into the biscotto, leaving Finn with the impression that she was using the time it took to chew and swallow to formulate a response.

"He knows both men. I guess you could say he traded on friendship."

"Lucky you."

She glanced out the window. "Yeah. Lucky me."

Now he was really curious. But he asked, "How did a chef with a degree from one of the best culinary schools in the country and who trained under a couple of Europe's finest chefs wind up making food look pretty on a plate for the camera?"

Her gaze snapped back to his. Her tone was mild, but her eyes held a bit of heat when she told him, "That's rather derogatory."

"The phrasing might be a little harsh," he allowed and took a sip of his coffee. "But it's a fact."

She was quiet a moment. Insulted? He didn't think so. But he'd definitely struck a nerve.

"Okaaay," she said slowly, drawing out the *a* as well as the suspense. He leaned forward slightly in his seat, drawn in and all but drowning in those green eyes. "Short answer?"

Finn found himself far more interested in the long version, but he nodded. He'd settle for that...for now.

"I sort of fell into it." She picked up her coffee.

That was it?

"You weren't kidding about offering a short answer." He took a sip from his mug before continuing, "I feel a little cheated. Come on. You can share more than that."

She made a humming noise. "I don't know that I should."

"Why not?"

"I'd rather be an enigma. A bit of mystery is good for... competition."

Funny, but competition was barely a blip on Finn's personal radar at the moment. He leaned forward. The neon sign wasn't the only thing buzzing right now.

"I have a proposition," he told her.

"Oh?" She appeared aloof, sitting there with her elbows on the table, both hands holding the coffee cup, which obscured his view of her mouth. But she leaned forward, too, bringing with her the appealing scent of vanilla and sweetness that he wasn't sure could be attributed to the hard Italian cookie. "What kind of a proposition?"

"The kind that involves physical contact," he replied. One of her elbows slipped off the tabletop, causing coffee to slosh over the rim of her mug. His ego fully stroked, he added, "I'm challenging you to another game of Rock, Paper, Scissors. Are you up for it?"

She sat back on a laugh. "Maybe. Depends."

"On?"

"What exactly does the winner get this time?"

Finn knew what he wanted, and it had nothing to do with spilling secrets or speaking at all. It did, however, involve her mouth. He swallowed.

"The long version." He coughed for effect. "I'm referring to answers."

"Gee, glad you clarified that." She grinned and looked away. "But I'm not sure what's in it for me, other than I get to keep a little of my mystique."

"You get to ask me a question of your choosing."

"Any question?"

Her eyes narrowed in a way he found worrisome. But Finn nodded. Being an enigma wasn't all that important to him. His name already had been dragged through the mud publicly. If she hadn't put it together yet, she would. Eventually.

"Sure. Any question. Well?"

"Deal." She clinked her coffee mug against his before setting it aside. Then she put out her hands. "On the count of three?"

This time when they finished, her fingers were curled in a fist for a rock. He'd gone with paper. Again. This time, he'd won.

"Paper covers rock." He cupped his palm over her fist, kept it there. The contact was warm, inviting.

"What do you want to know?" she asked quietly.

Finn thought about the questions he would like to have answered, including the one that she'd already evaded.

But what he asked was, "Are you seeing anyone?"

Are you seeing anyone?

That was what he wanted to know?

Was she flattered by Finn's interest? Check.

Turned on by it? Ditto.

Worried? *Ding! Ding! Ding!*

Concern topped the list, which was why she replied with a mood-killing "This…isn't a good time."

"For what?" he persisted. "I'm just trying to get the lay of the land. If you're seeing someone…" He put up his hands as he slouched back in his chair.

It was more for her own benefit than his that she told him, "I think we got off on the wrong foot."

"How so?" He looked genuinely confused, genuinely contrite. "Have I done or said anything to offend you?"

"No. Nothing."

In the very short time they'd known one another, Finn had done everything right, coming as close to perfect as any man ever had when measured against Lara's exacting post-divorce standards. And that made him dangerous. Especially right now.

"Here's the thing, Finn. I know where I stand with Ryder and Angel and the rest of the chefs in the competition. They'd poach my liver if they thought it would help their cause. But you…"

"My motives are suspect."

"No! Yes. I don't know." And she couldn't afford to find out.

"Well, at least you're sure." His accompanying grin took the sting out of his otherwise sarcastic reply.

She sighed. "I'm not making sense."

"It's okay. I think I know what you mean, Lara. The timing is wrong."

The timing was definitely wrong. How could she start a relationship with a man when she couldn't even be truthful with him about her last name?

She tried a second time to put into words what she herself barely understood.

"I really need to win."

"I know. I need it myself." He swallowed. "Nothing can...nothing *will* stand in the way."

They were on the same page, quoting practically the same verse. Leave it at that. But she didn't. Couldn't.

"I'm not seeing anyone, Finn. I haven't been seriously involved with anyone since... Well, in a long time. And I'd be lying if I claimed I don't find you attractive. But...let's just skip ahead to the bottom line."

Lara's fingers squeezed the ceramic mug until she wondered that it didn't shatter into tiny pieces. "I think it would be best if we stopped whatever is going on between us before it starts."

With her gaze glued to her half-eaten biscotto, she waited for him to argue with her. In fact, she found herself hoping he would.

But what Finn said was "You're right. Too much is at stake."

"Yes. For both of us."

After reaching that conclusion, they spent the next fifteen minutes awkwardly tripping over the elephant in the room as they attempted polite conversation and finished their coffees.

Finn picked up the tab. Lara plunked down a tip. Outside the shop, they stood in the muggy late-afternoon heat while she waited for a cab. When one finally sidled to the curb, they both reached for the handle. It was déjà vu, except for Finn's expression. His smile held no humor or bemusement. Only regret as oppressive as the humidity.

"Let me get the door for you," he said.

After she slid onto the seat, he didn't kiss her, but he did lean inside. "Rain check?"

"What?"

"If...*when* one of us is eliminated... What do you say? Rain check?"

"I… Okay." Holding back her grin, she added, "I'll take you out for drinks to commiserate when you've been voted off the show."

CHAPTER FIVE

Let marinate

"How did the other night go with your client?"

It was Friday and nearly time to knock off after a second long day of taping interviews that would air both on the television program and the show's website. Other than a couple of hellos, these were the first words Lara had said to him since coffee on Wednesday.

Finn didn't think she was ignoring him. The contestants had been kept extremely busy the past couple of days. And some of the taping they'd done had taken them away from the studio for several hours with their own camera crews.

Besides, after that bit of awkwardness at the coffee shop two days before, they'd left things on a friendly, flirty note.

He still wanted to give his forehead a thump over the question he'd asked her. Of all the things he could have had her clarify for him, her single status had topped the list?

Way to be subtle and smooth, Westbrook.

He wouldn't claim to be recovered from his divorce, even if he had moved on personally and was trying to do the same professionally. He doubted a person got over a betrayal like the one Sheryl and Cole had dealt him, first with their affair and later by cheating him out of his business.

But Finn felt good, relieved even, knowing he could feel

again. Even so, he remained a little off-kilter over his attraction for Lara.

She was wearing her hair back today, pulled into a neat ponytail at the base of her neck. The look could have made her appear no-nonsense or girlish even. But sexy? It was just Finn's bad luck that was how she struck him. He'd had a hard time concentrating whenever he'd caught a glimpse of her in the studio.

He'd always been a butt man, with legs coming a close second in terms of the body parts that drew his eye on a woman. In Lara's case, he liked everything, even her neck, which was long, slender, graceful and, thanks to the hairdo, accessible, as well.

"Finn?"

He realized he was staring. "Um, dinner. It went well. She had me prepare lamb chops for her guests."

"How many were there this time?"

"Seventeen. It was an intimate gathering for a change," he added wryly.

"Perhaps you should have gone into catering."

"Watch it, Scissors."

"I was a rock last time," she reminded him.

Finn shrugged. "Either way, you're getting nasty now."

But they both were smiling. Their gazes lingered as the silence turned conspicuous. She broke eye contact first.

"So, what are your plans for the weekend? And just so you know, I'm asking out of idle curiosity only. If I were standing next to Angel or Flo right now, I'd hit them with the same question."

"And if you were standing next to Ryder? What would you hit him with?"

"Funny. So?"

"Nothing too exciting. I'll probably just hang out in my apartment, watch a few movies, maybe catch up on episodes of my favorite sitcom on my DVR." She paused and cast Finn a sideways smile. "Oh, and cook amazing dishes under ridiculously tight timelines to get prepared for Monday. You?"

That streak of sass would be his undoing.

"The same. Except for the entertainment. Sitcoms are too fluffy for my taste. I'm more of a crime-drama guy. As for cooking, I have a job Saturday night."

"Oh? Is your client having another dinner party?"

"Actually, this is for someone else."

"Moonlighting, hmm?" Her brows lifted, disappearing into her bangs. Finn was sorely tempted to brush the hair aside. Her face was so pretty, he wanted to see all of it.

"I'm allowed."

"Yeah?" She made a humming sound. "That's interesting."

"How so?"

"I would have thought the setup with your Sugar Mommy was monogamous." Her lips twitched.

He chuckled, enjoying himself. "It's an open relationship. We're free to see other people."

The silence was back. This time it was more potent than moonshine.

"Chefs!" Tristan called as he came onto the soundstage where they'd been taping their interviews.

Clap! Clap! Clap!

The sound of his palms slapping together shattered the mood as effectively as fingernails down a chalkboard.

"How many times has he done that today?" Finn asked quietly.

"I think that makes six."

"Feels more like sixty."

"And every time he does it, he makes me feel like I'm about eight," she murmured.

"Before you leave today, don't forget to turn in your

chef coats," Tristan reminded them. "They will be here, pressed and waiting for you, first thing Monday morning."

All of the contestants had received identical crisp white jackets with their names embroidered in black thread on the left side of the chest. Finn noticed that Lara kept running her fingers over the stitching. In fact, she was doing it now. The gesture seemed born of nerves, which made sense. But there was something else going on, an undercurrent that he couldn't quite figure out.

"Well, I guess this is it."

"The last bit of peace before a full-fledged war breaks out?"

He meant it to be teasing, but she didn't smile. "Finn, no matter what happens, I—"

He stepped closer and stopped her words by laying a finger over her lips.

"See you next week. Bring your A game. You're going to need it."

The contestants who arrived at Sylvan Studios early Monday morning seemed different from the ones Finn had said goodbye to the previous Friday. As they huddled in the greenroom they were quieter, more introspective. Even Ryder was keeping his head down and his caustic comments to himself.

Finn was leaning against the far wall next to the coffeemaker, sipping from a disposable cup, when Lara arrived. He lifted his chin in acknowledgment, but other than that, he didn't say anything. Even when she crossed to where he stood and poured herself a cup of coffee, he remained silent.

Now was not the time for friendly chatter, much less sexually charged banter. It was game day and they were wearing their game faces. Someone, perhaps one of them, would be sent packing soon.

It was nearly two hours before they filed into the kitchen

studio dressed in their white chef coats. They'd been routed through makeup and wardrobe, and wired for sound. This marked the first time the contestants had been back inside since the previous week, when they'd been allowed one hour to acquaint themselves with their workstations. Today, the studio brimmed with people—dozens of camera operators and their various assistants, gaffers working the lights, boom operators positioning the microphones.

The ovens had been preheated. Water boiled in pots on all of the contestants' stoves. The oil in the deep fryers was at temperature. The pantry and refrigerator were fully stocked. Everything was ready, even if the contestants weren't.

Garrett St. John was on the set. The host's perfect smile looked even whiter against his tanned complexion. Someone from makeup was doing a touch-up, blotting at his suspiciously prominent cheekbones.

Finn glanced over at Lara. "Looking a little white there, Scissors. Maybe you need to sit down."

"I'm fine," she muttered. "Never better."

But her lips pinched together after saying so. It was to his advantage that she was nervous. Finn knew this. Nerves might cause her to make mistakes, leave out an ingredient or fail to plate her dish in time. He was here to win. He fully intended to win. But...

"You can always sit out this round. Meet me at Isadora's later. I'll buy you a coffee and biscotto."

His taunt did the trick. Her spine stiffened. When she glanced his way, some of the color had come back into her cheeks.

"You wish, Paper." She clasped her hands in front of her before turning them inside out and pretending to crack her knuckles. "Prepare to be dazzled."

She owed Finn.

He could have used her nerves against her. He'd talked

her down from the ledge instead. Yes, she owed him. But gratitude wouldn't keep her from winning.

Fifteen minutes later, she was ready, poised like a runner in the starting blocks, waiting for the red light to blink on and filming to begin.

It didn't.

Instead, Tristan came on the set. He clapped his damned hands.

"Chefs, your attention for a moment, please. Before we begin the competition, I have a surprise for you."

A surprise?

Generally speaking, Lara didn't mind surprises, but the excitement gleaming in Tristan's eyes gave her pause. This was something big. She sensed a game changer coming.

Apparently so did Finn.

"What the hell?" she heard him mutter half under his breath.

"I know you're eager to get started, but this will only take a minute. We have someone very special who wants to meet all of you."

Oh, no. No, no, no.

She chanted the denial in her head, even as Tristan pulled the rug out from under her feet by announcing, "Clifton Chesterfield, the owner of the landmark restaurant you are all hoping to run, is here today. Please give him a warm welcome."

"No!" Lara grabbed the edge of the prep table, willing herself to remain upright even as her meticulously laid plans crashed and burned around her.

He couldn't be here now. She hadn't proved anything yet.

"Are you all right?" Finn asked.

Dimly, she was aware of his hand on her waist, the pressure both welcome and reassuring. But she was too busy trying not to hyperventilate to reply.

"He's not supposed to be here," she finally managed.

She'd counted on that. Her father was a busy man. He wasn't supposed to come by the studio until the field of twelve contestants had been narrowed down to three. Tristan had confirmed that for Lara when she'd asked about it after surviving the preliminary rounds. Now that she was here, she planned to be one of the finalists, at which point, no matter what happened, she figured she would have proved herself.

"It's his restaurant. Why wouldn't he be here?" Finn sounded confused.

Before Lara could think of a reply, her father strode into the studio. Clifton hadn't changed much over the years, although his auburn hair was shot through with silver at his temples, and it looked a little thinner on top. The beard was new. Neatly trimmed and accompanied by a mustache, it framed his face and served to camouflage his full cheeks. It, too, was streaked with gray. The lines that fanned out from his eyes were deeper than she remembered, as were the ones that bracketed his mouth, but her father would be turning sixty-five this year. He might like to believe himself omnipotent, but even he couldn't stop time.

Or heart disease. The attack he'd suffered a year ago had been mild, but according to her aunt, the doctors were clear that he needed to change his lifestyle if he intended to live to a ripe old age.

In the meantime, he was shoring up his legacy. He was choosing not only his successor, with this competition, but potentially his heir. Her heart sank. She'd planned to earn his approval by competing. That wasn't likely to happen now.

"Greetings, chefs," he called out in the booming voice she remembered from her childhood. "I hadn't planned to make your acquaintance until later in the competition, when only the best of the very best would still be here, but

I had a little free time in my schedule today and I wanted to surprise you."

In lieu of the maroon chef's coat he wore while presiding over the Chesterfield's kitchen, he had on a suit that was impeccably tailored to accommodate both his height and his substantial girth. Lara swallowed and fussed with her bangs, wishing they were longer and could hide her from view. But she knew her moment of reckoning was coming soon.

"I wanted to see for myself the caliber of the candidates the network pulled together from across the country. So, you twelve chefs think you are up to the Chesterfield's exacting standards?"

He folded his arms over his chest as he spoke and scanned the room. His laserlike gaze touched briefly on each competitor, assessing them. When he got to her, he blinked twice.

"Lara?" The disbelieving tone lasted only a moment. In that scant second she wanted to believe he was happy to see her. The prodigal daughter returning to the fold. Then disbelief gave way to something darker. Oh, this look she remembered well. Irritation. Anger. Disappointment. No fatted calf would be killed to celebrate her homecoming.

Clifton shouted at Garrett, "What is the meaning of this? What is she doing here?"

"I—I don't understand," the host stammered.

Her father glanced around. "Is this someone's idea of a joke?"

Even as Garrett stepped out of her father's line of fire, Tristan was stepping forward.

Poor Tristan. He didn't have a clue about what was going on, so he argued, "I've tasted some of her dishes myself. I can assure you, she knows what she's doing. She wouldn't have gotten this far in the competition if she didn't. She had to beat some amazing talent to be standing where she is."

The younger man's words were balm to her battered soul. Under other circumstances, they would have been enough to dispel any doubts. But with her father glowering at her in much the same manner as he had the last time they'd spoken in person, it was impossible to feel completely reassured.

"I want to know what she is doing here," Clifton demanded a second time.

Lara glanced at Finn, who had yet to remove his hand from the small of her back. Taking comfort from that, she swallowed and stepped into range of her father's legendary temper, hoping to calm him down before he got too irate. Elevated blood pressure wasn't good for a man with his medical problems.

"I'm here to compete with everyone else for a chance to run your kitchen."

He snorted. "You had your chance. You threw it away."

"Yes, I threw it away," she admitted. She tipped up her chin. Her father respected strength. Groveling would get her nowhere.

"Yet you have the nerve to show up here now."

"I didn't just show up," she argued. "I'm here to compete. As Tristan said, I *earned* the right."

"A *food stylist*?"

Her father's tone was a verbal slap that left her stinging. Finn's hand, meanwhile, tightened. Was he recalling his own derogatory tone from the other day when they'd discussed her profession?

"She did, Mr. Chesterfield." Tristan nodded so vigorously he reminded her of a bobblehead doll. "I can attest to that. Lara Smith won all of the challenges required of the contestants in order to be here. She made it to the top twelve on her own merit."

"Except that she isn't Lara Smith."

"Excuse me?"

"Good God!" Clifton thundered. "You really don't know who she is?"

The set was alive now with murmured speculation. The gazes of not only the contestants, but everyone from the members of the sound crew to the lighting technicians to the lanky young men who were hauling around the camera cables—all were trained on her. And then there was Finn, standing quietly at her side, hand still on her waist. But for how much longer?

For someone who had never cared to be the center of attention, Lara was now. While she might wish for privacy for this unhappy family reunion, she'd known she would be giving up that luxury when she'd tried out for the show.

"Her name is Lara Dunham," her father continued. "Before she married the bastard food critic who had the nerve to give my restaurant the one and only two-star rating it's ever received, she was Lara Chesterfield."

"Chesterfield!" Tristan squeaked. He was a small man. Under her father's penetrating glare, he seemed to shrink.

Although it was unnecessary, Clifton declared, "She's my daughter."

Finn's hand fell away at her unmasking. Along with everyone else, he stared at her. Gaped, really, the way one did when viewing a particularly nasty car accident.

"Lara Dunham," she heard him say as if testing out her name on his tongue. She liked hearing him say it, even if he did so in a hushed tone that rang with accusation.

Her father's was demanding. "What do you have to say for yourself?"

"I think my presence here says it all," she told him with more dignity and calmness than she actually felt.

"You don't belong here," her father replied.

"I beg to differ."

"You had your chance. You blew it."

She wouldn't argue with him on that score, but she

needed to make one thing clear. "I'm not asking for a chance to run your kitchen based on who I am. As you said, I blew it. I'm asking for a chance to compete for the executive-chef job like everyone else. It's what I've been doing."

Tristan cleared his throat. "I can confirm that the judges have shown no favoritism. She's gotten to this point on merit and merit alone. No one knew who she was."

"I won't have it!"

"Sir—"

"No!"

With that single syllable, she knew that her hopes were dashed.

"Stick a fork in her. She's done." Even as a whisper, Ryder's gravelly tone was unmistakable.

The guy was a jerk, but that didn't make him any less right. She'd been outed as Clifton's daughter, exposed as a liar who had entered the contest under a fraudulent name. She might have hoped for a different outcome, but that didn't change the facts. She was off the show.

"Excuse me," she said.

She would not cry. Not here. Not in front of the other contestants. And especially not in front of her father, whose hostility was as painful as his lack of faith in her abilities. Head held high, she started for the door.

"I guess we know who the first to be eliminated is," Ryder said as she passed his workstation. His tone mirrored her father's when he sneered, "The food stylist."

"Quit being an ass," Finn snarled.

CHAPTER SIX

Puree

LARA DUNHAM. THAT was her name. Not Lara Smith.

And she was a liar.

Even as Finn processed that thought, he wanted to dismiss it. Yes, Lara had lied to him and everyone else here, but her motives were different than his ex-wife's and that had to count for something. Didn't it?

But betrayal, even one not intended for him, still left a sour taste in his mouth. As irritated as he was, however, he also was curious. Why had she done it?

Answers, unfortunately, were not forthcoming.

After Lara's unmasking, all hell pretty much had broken loose on the set. Men and women dressed in conservative attire arrived en masse. Lawyers and the folks who ran the business side of things, Finn assumed. None of them had looked pleased with the new development.

At the producer's urging, the studio was cleared and Tristan sent the contestants to the greenroom to wait. That was where they were now, making do with stale coffee and the hard Danishes left over from that morning.

Where the greenroom had been unnaturally quiet earlier, it was alive with speculation now.

"I wonder if they'll bring back a contestant from one of the preliminary rounds," Flo pondered aloud.

"I smell a lawsuit coming from the chefs who got elim-inated in the early rounds she competed in," Angel said.

On and on it went until Finn, tired of their theories and conjecture, broke his silence.

"We'll find out soon enough. There's nothing to do now but wait."

"Missing your girlfriend?" Ryder grinned like a Viking who'd just plundered his first village.

Lara wasn't Finn's girlfriend and he wasn't missing her... exactly. But the barb struck a nerve nonetheless. Something had passed between them starting at their first accidental meeting, a stubborn spark of attraction that had continued to burn even after they'd learned they were quasi-adversaries, both after the same thing. Her lies should have snuffed out that spark for good, but knowing that they were no longer on opposing sides had him keyed up, confused.

What was going to happen now? The question echoing through his head had nothing to do with the competition. And, yeah, that irritated him.

"I just don't see the point in speculating."

"Well, I do." Then, to no one in particular, Ryder said, "If you ask me, they'd be smart to go ahead with just the eleven of us."

"They can't do that." Kirby's reply was met with a cou-ple of nods and murmured agreements.

"Why the hell not?" Ryder challenged.

"I..." Kirby shrugged before running a hand through his hair, leaving his mangled locks more disheveled than before.

Ryder continued. "Don't tell me someone at the network didn't know who Lara really was. Someone got paid off to let her into the finals."

Angel and some of the other chefs were nodding, but Finn wasn't buying it. The surprise all around had been too genuine to be manufactured. And the cover-your-ass efforts the network was currently employing underscored that fact. Lara had pulled the wool over everyone's eyes. Of that much, Finn was certain.

So, he tuned out Ryder and the rest of the contestants, and sat in the corner of the greenroom nursing a cup of coffee that had grown bitter and cold.

Finally, nearly four hours after the debacle in the kitchen had unfolded, Tristan stopped in to tell them that the judges had been sent home and filming would not take place after all. In fact, the competition would not resume for a week, possibly longer, while everything was sorted out.

"What's going to happen to Lara's spot?" someone asked.

"We're not sure. We'll have answers for you as soon as possible," Tristan assured them. "In the meantime, use the time off to relax, and, as a token of our appreciation for your patience, we are giving you all tickets to a Broadway production. Stop by the reception desk and see Evelyn for details."

Only one person could answer Finn's questions, and it didn't look as if he would be seeing her again. He knew her true identity now, but he didn't have her number. Nor did he know where she lived. He wasn't sure how he felt about that.

Officially, of course, Tristan hadn't confirmed that she was off the show, but her own father wanted her gone, so it seemed a done deal. Besides, Finn figured the network couldn't allow her to stay on without risking having viewers think the outcome was rigged and not bothering to tune in. As it was, the lawyers were no doubt earning their keep trying to figure out a way to prevent this from blowing up in the network's face.

Liars and cheats.

Finn had had his fill of both. Still, when he saw Lara outside, waiting for a cab, his pulse quickened, and before he could decide if it were wise, he closed the distance to where she stood.

"Rough day?" he inquired once he was within earshot.

She started at the sound of his voice. When she turned, the expression on her face was a combination of regret, embarrassment and that guilt he'd spied a time or two already. At least now he understood its source.

"Let's just say I've had better. No one is very happy with me right now. Not the network, not the people affiliated with the show and certainly not my father."

"Did you expect them to be?"

"No." She swallowed. "I suppose you're not all that pleased with me either."

"Gee, *Miz Smith*," he drawled, "what gave you that impression?"

"If it counts for anything, I didn't like lying to you, especially about my name."

Did it count? Finn had been the casualty of too many lies in the past to be sure.

"But the end justifies the means?"

"I guess I thought so. But I've been wrong about a lot of things, especially where my father is concerned." She reached out and her fingers grazed his arm. Her touch was light, the effect on his skin akin to that of a cattle prod. "I am sorry, Finn."

He nodded stiffly, still on the fence. Wavering or not, though, he had to ask, "Why did you do it? It's none of my business, and you don't have to tell me, but I can't help being curious."

"Why did I enter the contest?"

"Yeah. You had to have known that, sooner or later, you would be found out. I mean, Clifton Chesterfield is your father. So…why?"

"The million-dollar question." Her smile was sad and

about as forthcoming as her answer. The laughter that accompanied it was humorless.

Finn reached into the front pocket of his pants and pulled out the change from the coffee he'd purchased on his way over that morning.

"Sorry. I've only got six bucks and some coins. It's enough to buy a decent cup of Colombian and one macadamia-nut-and-dried-cranberry biscotto."

She blinked. The beginnings of a smile tugged at her lips. "Are you offering to buy me a cup of coffee?"

"No."

Smile aborted, she started to turn away. Finn caught her arm. "I think *you* should buy *me* a cup."

She tilted her head to one side. "Why?"

Why indeed? Rather than mention that he found her attractive and wouldn't mind spending a little more time in her company, he went with the most obvious answer.

"I bought the last one."

"Isadora's?" she asked.

"Is there any place else?"

Lara had planned to go home and drown her sorrows in a hot bubble bath, maybe while drinking a couple of glasses of wine and indulging in some dark chocolate. Coffee with a side of sexy man held a lot more appeal. As for having to pick up the tab for the beverages and biscotti, that seemed a small price to pay.

Half an hour later, they were seated at the same table they'd occupied the previous week waiting for the same young woman to bring them their order.

Lara had stalled long enough. "So, I guess you're waiting to hear my reasons for entering the contest."

"That's right."

Fair enough, she thought. But she replied, "A little background first. My father and I…we don't have an ideal relationship, as you probably noticed."

Finn nodded. "It was kind of hard to miss. Has it always been that way?"

"Not as bad as it is now, but I've never just been his daughter. I've always felt like a blob of dough he's been kneading to get just right before he puts it in the oven."

"And you've rebelled," Finn said, apparently recalling her earlier remark.

She nodded. "Dad pushed me into the culinary arts from the time I could walk. I knew the difference between searing and sautéing by the age of four, and made my first béchamel when I was six." Her tone turned wry. "My father thought my white sauce was too thick. He threw it out and made me redo it three times before he was satisfied."

"That's rough."

"He's a hard man to please."

She frowned at the memories that accompanied her words. While other kids had been outside learning to ride their bikes or playing in the park with friends, she'd been in the kitchen, either at their home or, more often than not, at the restaurant. Never could she recall earning her father's unqualified praise. Every compliment was tempered with criticism.

Your pork is well seasoned and grilled to perfection, but the portion is too small and the plating is sloppy.

Comments such as that one, which she'd received for the Father's Day dinner she'd made him when she was twelve, still rang in her head.

It was no wonder Finn's brow creased in confusion when he said, "Yet you wanted to work for him. For that matter, you've gone to a lot of trouble for the mere opportunity to labor in his kitchen."

Lara didn't mention that as executive chef she would

have been at th

moot. And Finn w

But she couldn't

for him, too."

Finn's broad shoulders

ing restaurant owners and ch

a guy who threw an entire pot

head because a customer complain

A lot of people in our industry are te

acting. Besides, working at your fathe

means to an end in my case. I don't plan to

at the Chesterfield. A year—two, tops."

"A means to an end, hmm?" Didn't that soun

And much more interesting than her current family

She propped her elbows on the table and rested her ch

her palms. "Do tell."

"Nice try." But he shook his head and asked point-blank,
"Why do you want to work for your father?"

"Well, like you, I saw it as a means to an end. I'm not
sure I planned to make a career of it either."

"How can you *not* be sure?"

"It's complicated." The waitress arrived with their coffees and biscotti. Lara took a sip of the steaming beverage
before telling Finn, "My father had a heart attack last year."

He blinked in surprise. "I didn't know."

"It's not common knowledge. Anyway, it was a mild
one, but it served as a wake-up call, especially for me."

Indeed, if Lara had learned anything over the past year,
it was that life was short and time was marching on. Her
parents were getting older. Their health wasn't what it
once was. And the unresolved baggage she'd been carrying around since childhood had grown so heavy, so un-
wieldy, that it had left her all but immobilized.

"He was in the hospital for less than a week. From what
my aunt has told me, he's supposed to be working fewer

e top of the pecking order. The point was
s right. She *had* gone to a lot of trouble.
elp pointing out, "You want to work

fted. "I've worked for demand-
efs before. I once worked for
of mashed potatoes at my
d they were too lumpy.
mperamental and ex-
's restaurant is a
make a career

d cryptic?
drama.
n on

...guests. It's where he spent all of his weekends and every holiday of my childhood with the exception of Christmas. The Chesterfield was closed on Christmas Day. Otherwise, I'm pretty sure he would have spent that one there, too."

"Long hours are to be expected. You know that. Especially for someone who both owns the restaurant and runs the kitchen. That's the nature of the business."

"I don't buy that," Lara replied. "At first, yes. But twenty years after Dad opened the Chesterfield, even when he had other capable chefs on his payroll, it was the same. He wouldn't even take a vacation.

"He and my mother argued a lot because of his priorities. Number one was the restaurant. *Always* the restaurant. She thought his family should come first."

Lara, who felt she fell far down on the priority lists of *both* of her parents, agreed.

"How old were you when they split up?" Finn asked.

"Oh, I was an adult." Lara's lips twisted briefly into a frown. "I'm not sure she did me any favors by sticking it out that long. We were a broken family long before she left and they called it quits.

"I was in Europe, studying under one of Dad's protégés, when she packed her bags. By the time I got back, she'd moved clear across the country."

Lara swallowed, recalling how gutted she'd felt at the time. She might have been an adult, but that hadn't kept her from feeling abandoned, and, yes, she'd taken that out on her dad, too.

"I'm sorry."

Finn's quiet compassion made her throat ache. When he reached across the table and brushed his fingertips over her arm, it was all she could do to hold back her tears. She hadn't felt this vulnerable, or this connected, in a long time. The vulnerability in particular didn't sit well. So, she worked up a look of nonchalance and, on a shrug, replied. "It's ancient history. I'm over it."

A pair of gray eyes regarded her intently. Even though Finn didn't say anything, she got the feeling he knew that she was lying. She looked away first.

With her gaze on the pedestrians marching along Forty-Eighth Street, she said, "Anyway, I can't say I blame her for being tired of playing second fiddle to the restaurant." Lara had been tired of it, too, which really had been the point of her rebellion. "In fairness to my father, Mom was no picnic to live with either. She was and remains a frustrated writer."

"Is that another way of saying she is unpublished?"

Lara snorted out a laugh and nodded. "To my knowledge, she hasn't ever finished a manuscript. She just keeps polishing the first few chapters of the same one she started writing when I was in high school. It's about the murder of a prominent chef," she added drily.

"Maybe it's a good thing that she's never finished it, then."

The smile that accompanied his words had one tugging at her lips in response.

"Maybe." She exhaled. "Anyway, we've all pretty much lived separate lives for several years. I was already starting to regret the rift with my father when he had his heart attack."

"Adversity has a way of bringing families together."

His wry expression made it seem as if he was speaking from firsthand experience, but he was making a winding motion with his finger, urging her to go on, so she didn't ask.

"When my mother heard about it, she had second thoughts, not only about the estrangement between me and her, but the rift between my father and me. She didn't overtly encourage it, but she said things, both before and after the divorce, that put my dad in a less-than-positive light."

"So, she suffered a crisis of conscience, realized life is too short to hold a grudge and encouraged you to make amends."

"Something like that." Lara dipped the biscotto into her coffee and took another bite. "She was the one who encouraged me to sign up for the show after my previous attempts to reconnect with my dad went nowhere. It seemed like a good idea at the time."

"So, you don't have any brothers or sisters, I take it."

"Nope. Just me, the lucky only child."

While her parents hadn't done the greatest job in the world of raising her, the fact remained that they were all she had.

"That's rough. I've got a couple of sisters, both younger." One side of his mouth quirked up. "While we were growing up, I thought they were a pain in the ass, but now that we're adults, I've come to appreciate them." His tone turned thoughtful. "They have a way of showing up when I need them the most."

"That's nice. I have a friend like that," Lara replied, thinking of Dana Heartland, who lived in an apartment just down the hall. "She's like a sister, in many ways. And she's been after me to make up with my father, too."

Finn leaned forward in his seat. "Is your relationship with your dad so strained that you couldn't just, I don't know, pick up the phone and call him?"

If only it were that easy. She shook her head, sad again.

"I burned a lot of bridges over the years."

"Still…" Finn looked doubtful.

"You saw him today. Every attempt I've made to contact him has been met with pretty much the same result. He's had me thrown out of his restaurant. He even had security escort me from the hospital when I tried to visit after his heart attack," she admitted with no small amount of embarrassment. "He hangs up when I call. He's told mutual friends that he doesn't have a daughter."

Finn muttered an oath. "That's harsh."

"Yeah, well, I deserve it," Lara admitted quietly.

But Finn shook his head, gray eyes narrowed in fierce disagreement. "No. No one deserves that kind of treatment from their own father, Lara."

She swallowed as his face grew blurry in her vision, and she hugged Finn's words close, wanting to believe them even though she knew she had given her dad plenty of reasons over the years to sever all ties.

The upbringing Lara described was sad, tragic even, and the polar opposite of his own. For Finn, childhood had been happy and relatively free of drama despite those two younger sisters he'd mentioned. Sisters who, like the rest of his family, had been there to pick him up after betrayal and divorce had kicked the foundation out from beneath him.

Across the table, Lara's eyes were bright and focused on her coffee. She blinked rapidly, doing her damnedest to hold it together, and made a show of using her index finger to pick up errant crumbs from the scarred Formica tabletop. Her attempt at nonchalance wasn't fooling him one bit. The day's events had taken an emotional toll.

She hadn't entered the contest only to make reparations with her father. Oh, Finn didn't doubt that Clifton's heart attack had prompted some soul-searching and remorse on her part. Facing mortality did that. But she had another reason, too. One she hadn't mentioned and might not even realize was driving her.

Lara Dunham wanted her father's approval.

After all, what kid, even as an adult, didn't crave a parent's endorsement?

Finn knew what his folks' praise and encouragement had meant to him over the years. Not only had they scrimped and saved to send him to culinary school, but they'd also taken out a second mortgage on their duplex in Queens to help him open his restaurant. Over the years, their pride and support had never wavered—not when Finn married Sheryl despite their reservations, nor when she'd raked his reputation over the coals by claiming ownership of his recipes. Hell, especially then, he'd been able to count on them. They'd remained firmly in his corner, and were there today, always ready to root him on.

Given Lara's glum expression, he decided it was time to change the subject. He still had more questions he wanted answered. Indeed, his curiosity, among other things, was far from satisfied. But another time, another place.

She needed some cheering up, and while coffee and biscotti were a good start, he knew another way.

"Hey, we've got the afternoon free. Want to spend it together?"

"Doing what exactly?"

Her lips puckered ever so slightly as she asked the question. Finn lost his train of thought and nearly suggested an activity far more intimate than the one he had been considering.

Another time, another place, he reminded himself.

"Ever fly a kite?" he asked.

CHAPTER SEVEN

Preheat oven

THE AFTERNOON SUN glared down from a hazy blue sky brushed with clouds that reminded Lara of cotton batting that had been stretched too thin.

She couldn't recall the last time she'd spent any length of time in Central Park, unless it was to jog on the path that circled the reservoir. Yet here she was with Finn, on what was arguably one of the worst days of her life, flying a kite.

Or, more accurately, trying to. The kite in question was currently lodged in the high branches of an uncooperative oak tree.

She and Finn had purchased it at a party store near Grand Army Plaza. He'd left it to her to pick the design. She'd gone with a butterfly whose brightly colored wings carried a cheerful vibe. Nothing about them was cheerful now that they were bent at odd angles while the kite dangled from its perch. Every now and then the breeze caught it and it would flutter maniacally, only making matters worse. Lara could relate.

"It's hopeless," she told him.

"It's not." Undeterred, he handed her the spool of string. "I'll just go up and get it."

Climbing the tree wasn't as easy as he made it sound. The lowest branch was a good nine feet off the ground, re-

quiring him to jump to reach it. He managed to grab hold
on the second try. He dangled in midair for a moment, legs
kicking while he wrapped his arms more securely around
its width. His shirt came untucked in the process, giving
Lara a tantalizing view of taut abs bisected by a dusting of
dark hair that disappeared into the waistband of his khakis. Her gaze was on his belt buckle, inappropriate thoughts
percolating away, as he tried to hoist a leg over the branch.
He lost his hold and crashed to the ground.

"Finn!" She rushed to where he lay on the grass. "Oh,
my God! Are you hurt?"

"Only my pride." He grunted and pushed up on one
elbow. "I used to be able to climb trees with the best of
them. I guess I'm out of shape."

Based on what she'd seen, Lara begged to differ.

"It looks like our kite-flying expedition is over," he told
her.

She glanced momentarily at the butterfly tangled in the
boughs overhead. It still looked pathetic, but she was no
longer feeling that way herself.

"I appreciate you trying." She touched his temple on
the pretext of brushing away dirt. "I appreciate everything
you've done today."

"You bought the coffee," he pointed out.

"You know what I mean."

His expression sobered. "Yeah, I do."

Finn didn't bother with pretext. He wanted to touch Lara
and so he did. After pulling himself up to a sitting position, he took her face between his hands and kissed her.

It wasn't intended to be a rock-your-world kiss. The sort
that got the party started when it came to physical attraction. The fact that it was? Well, he considered that a happy
coincidence. He was just trying to satisfy his curiosity.
Had their previous kiss really been as good as he recalled?

The answer was an immediate and resounding *Yes!*

"I thought I might have imagined that," he murmured against her lips.

"Imagined what?"

"The…sizzle."

Her laughter was low, personal. "I know. Me, too."

She maneuvered back a little and plucked at the grass. Given her show of restraint, when she asked, "So, what do you want to do now?" Finn figured that wasn't code for "Let's go get hot and sweaty at my place."

And because he wanted to get hot and sweaty with Lara, whether at her place or his, he pushed to his feet and offered her his hand.

"Let's go get ice cream."

They spent the next two hours walking around Central Park with no actual destination in mind and all but oblivious to the joggers, cyclists and baby-stroller-pushing nannies they passed along the way. At one point, Finn had taken her hand, pulling her away from a spot on the asphalt where someone had spat out a wad of chewing gum that was now gooey from the heat. After saving her shoe from certain disaster, however, he'd kept her hand tucked in his.

Sizzle. It was there even in this simple connection.

"I've got a question for you," she said as they wound their way past Belvedere Castle.

Turnabout was fair play, so he told her, "Shoot."

"You obviously have talent as a chef. And you've already told me you don't plan to make a career out of working for my father, so…"

"Why do I want to work there?"

She nodded.

"I used to have a restaurant. I…lost it."

"Sorry," she told him. "The economy hurt a lot of establishments."

Lara was assuming his restaurant had gone under, a casualty of the recession. Finn didn't correct her. He wasn't being purposely evasive. Rather, he didn't see the point of trotting out the details of his divorce right now. They were too humiliating.

"I want to open another place. In the interim, a job with some prestige wouldn't hurt."

"You don't consider being a personal chef for wealthy clients prestigious?"

"Selling my services to the highest bidder, you mean?" he teased.

"I'm never going to live that down, am I?"

"Nope." But he grinned. "To answer your question, being a personal chef holds some cachet and it certainly pays the bills."

In fact, it did so nicely thanks to his current client list. During the past several months, Finn had been able to sock away a decent amount of savings. While he was a long way from being able to finance his own place, it was a start.

"But it's not the same as running a restaurant kitchen," she surmised.

"Exactly. Nothing else compares."

Lara nodded. "What do you miss most about it?"

Finn missed everything, but if he had to pick one thing it was this memory as he replied, "The tickets pouring in during the dinner rush. Then the expeditor coming back and calling out the orders. It's chaotic and exciting at the same time trying to meet the demand and get the food out as quickly as possible."

"I haven't worked in a restaurant in ages, but I loved it when I saw cleaned plates being cleared from the tables."

"Nothing worse than wasted food because customers didn't like what was served," he agreed.

They emerged on Central Park West a few minutes later. He raised their clasped hands so he could see his watch. Then he swore softly at the time.

"It's later than I thought."

"And you have someplace you need to be," Lara added.

"I do, yes."

"A job?"

"Family. I promised my mother I'd come for dinner. She said she'd hold it as long as necessary. She and my sisters will want all of the juicy details from today." He closed one eye and grimaced. "What I mean is, they don't know the competition has been postponed. They're still waiting to hear who got sent home."

He grimaced again. "Sorry."

"It's okay. I know what you mean." Her fingers slipped from his, and she fiddled with her hair, pushing it back behind one ear. "I appreciate all of the time you spent with me today."

"It wasn't exactly a hardship."

She smiled. "Despite the kite mishap?"

"Despite that." He grew serious. "It's going to be okay, Lara. You'll find a way to fix things with your father. I think he already knows you're a credible chef. He's probably just having a hard time admitting it. And if you are serious about a career change, well, I'm sure you'll manage that, too."

"Thanks." She nodded, but she appeared far from convinced.

He touched her cheek. "Persistence. It's what's gotten you this far, right?"

"Right."

Time was tight, but Finn couldn't leave without one last kiss.

"Isadora's tomorrow morning?" he asked, as he raised his arm to hail a cab.

"Is seven too early for you?" she said in reply.

"I'll set an alarm." Seeing Lara first thing would be worth a short night's sleep.

A taxi pulled to the curb as they exchanged cell numbers.

"Thanks again for saving my day from being a total

disaster. It had all the markings of it after the scene with my father."

Finn brushed aside her gratitude. He'd gotten as much as he'd given, he figured. He couldn't recall the last time he'd cleared his agenda and spent the day in the park.

He pulled her close for another kiss that he was forced to keep brief because the cabdriver was eyeing them impatiently. Even so, he found himself thinking about that kiss—and the satisfied look on Lara's face afterward—for the remainder of the evening.

"I'm sorry, Lara. I know how much this meant to you," her friend Dana said.

They were seated on the couch in Lara's meagerly proportioned walk-up, bare feet tucked up beneath them and wallowing in the pint of ice cream Dana had so thoughtfully brought for the occasion.

Her friend was a struggling actress—emphasis on *struggling*. Dana currently had a small role in a stage production that was so far off Broadway it might as well have been in New Jersey. Yet she was always there for Lara, ready to help soothe heartache with some mint chocolate chip.

"I should have gotten the half gallon," Dana mused.

"I'm glad you didn't. This is my second serving of ice cream today."

Dana licked her spoon. "Second?"

"I spent time in the park. We flew a kite." Her mouth crooked with a smile as she thought about the plastic butterfly's fate in the branches of the oak.

"We? I assume from the look on your face the other half of that *We* was male."

"One hundred percent, certified prime," Lara confirmed. Thinking of Finn's wry sense of humor, sexy eyes and that peek she'd gotten of washboard abs, she sighed.

"Uh-oh."

"What?"

"I haven't heard you sigh over a man since... Well, I don't think I've ever heard you sigh over a man."

Lara spooned up more ice cream. "Really?"

"Really. Where did you meet him? When?"

"Aren't you full of questions," Lara chided.

"Living vicariously. Now spill."

"Okay. We met outside the magazine offices where I styled food for a shoot last week. I was on my way to the network's kitchens. We both went for the same cab."

"And you shared it," her friend surmised with a sappy grin.

"No. We played Rock, Paper, Scissors for it." Lara savored both the ice cream and the memory.

"Um, is that supposed to be romantic?"

"Actually, at the time, it was intended to be practical. I won and got in the cab just before it started pouring. He wound up getting soaked. Then, after I got to the studio, who walks in a few minutes later?"

"Cab guy. Um, does he have a name?"

"Finn Westbrook."

"Finn Westbrook. Hmm, that sounds familiar."

"Yeah?" Lara scratched her cheek.

"Obviously, he's a chef. Has he appeared on some of the Cuisine Cable Network's other programs? I swear that woman with the over-the-top Boston accent was on two or three different competition shows before she wound up with her own. *Dinnah with Dinah*." Dana rolled her eyes.

"I don't think so," Lara replied. "But I don't watch a lot of television." She'd rather spend time cooking than watch someone else doing it. "I thought his name seemed a little familiar, too, but I would have remembered his face if I'd seen it before."

Dana grinned and inquired, "That good-looking?"

In response, Lara filled her mouth with another spoonful of ice cream and offered a smugly satisfied "Mmm."

"I'd be jealous if I had time for a man right now, which I

don't." Having said that, Dana then shook her head. "Forget it. I am jealous. It's all so *Romeo and Juliet.*" She sighed. "Star-crossed chefs, both competing for the same prize. Maybe it's fate that your father showed up when he did so that you and Finn aren't pitted against one another."

"It wouldn't have mattered. We had already agreed to see one another, although we'd decided to wait until one of us was off the show. That just happened sooner than I anticipated." Lara frowned again. "A lot sooner."

"Well, at least your day from hell has a silver lining," her friend reminded her.

It did at that.

"We're meeting tomorrow morning at Isadora's. It turns out he's a regular there, too. Although he usually comes in a lot later in the morning than I do. He's a personal chef right now, making meals for wealthy Park Avenue types. But he wants to run his own kitchen, and he sees winning this competition as a stepping-stone to doing that."

Dana cleared her throat. "Not to rain on your parade, but, um, have you given any thought to what you're going to do if Finn does win?"

"What do you mean?"

"Obviously, you want to keep seeing him, but how are you going to feel if he winds up with the job you wanted? He'll be your father's successor, Lara. Not you."

She swallowed. "As I said, Finn sees it as a stepping-stone."

"Okay," Dana replied, but her tone held a note of uncertainty that rippled into Lara's good mood.

How *was* she going to feel?

CHAPTER EIGHT

Sauté

WHEN LARA ARRIVED at Isadora's the following morning, Finn was sitting by the window at the table she'd already come to think of as theirs.

She was surprised that he'd arrived first, since she was the early riser and he'd already admitted to sleeping in on a regular basis. But he was jotting down notes, a half-empty cup of coffee on the table in front of him.

Since he hadn't seen her yet, she took a moment to relish the sight of him. The man was gorgeous and every bit as mouthwatering as the biscotti for which Isadora's was famous. He was wearing faded jeans and a logoed T-shirt that had seen better days. His sandy hair was tousled and stubble shadowed his jaw, but he looked sexy rather than unkempt.

He glanced up then and their gazes met. Awareness arced between them like an electrical current.

"Good morning," she managed.

Finn smiled. "Morning." He motioned toward his coffee cup. "Hope you don't mind, but I went ahead and ordered without you."

"That's okay." She slipped onto the chair opposite his. "How long have you been here?"

"Since they opened at six."

His answer had her blinking in surprise. "Six o'clock? What got you out of bed so early?"

"You."

Her pulse rate shot up right along with the corners of his mouth. His smile was pure sin.

"Me?"

"I couldn't sleep. I was thinking about you…and food."

"I'm flattered. I think." She laughed. "I guess I hoped to inspire more than insomnia and binge eating."

"Oh, you have. Trust me."

And there was that grin again. It was a good thing she was seated or Lara figured her knees would have given out. It was that potent.

He was saying, "Desserts aren't my forte, but I got the idea for a very decadent cake."

"Chocolate?"

"Is there any other kind of decadent?" he asked.

"Sounds good." She peeked over at his notebook, but he closed it before she could read anything.

"I'll make it for you sometime," he promised as the waitress came over to take Lara's order.

"So, how did dinner with your family go last night?" she asked when they were alone again.

"Good. Dad broke out the good Scotch and Mom made her famous lasagna."

"Famous?"

Oddly, his expression clouded at that. "The sauce she uses is an old family recipe."

Lara nodded, although she wasn't sure why that should have him frowning.

"I assume you told them about, well, everything that transpired yesterday."

"Not *everything*. I decided it best to leave a few parts out." He winked.

"Oh?" Gooseflesh pricked her flesh at the memory of what she thought those parts might be.

"Yeah, I'd never live it down if my sisters knew I fell out of a tree."

Lara laughed.

Across the room, a commotion involving a young couple broke out. Lara wasn't sure what was going on, but the woman was on her feet now, calling the man a few choice names. Then she pulled a ring from her finger, and tossed it and her iced coffee in his face before storming out of the shop. Her embarrassed suitor left soon after.

"That was ugly," Lara noted.

"I had something similar happen."

"To you?"

"To a client for whom I had cooked an intimate dinner during which he planned to propose to his girlfriend of three years. And more than beverages got tossed."

"A food fight?" She found the idea both fascinating and appalling.

Finn nodded. "His plan blew up in his face when she confronted him about sleeping with her sister."

"Ooh. What a jerk."

"I thought so, too. Which is why I handed her the lemon-meringue pie when she was looking for something to throw at him."

"You did not." Lara gaped at Finn, more amazed than scandalized.

"It seemed fitting since he had me put the engagement ring in the pie. He was going to make sure she got the slice with the diamond, and then, when she found it, he was going to pop the question."

Lara nibbled the inside of her cheek. "Still, it seems like a waste of a good pie."

"The meringue was one of my best." Finn frowned. His tone wasn't as circumspect as his words when he said, "I don't get why people cheat, especially with someone like a sister or close friend. That kind of betrayal…"

"Yeah. It would cut even deeper."

"Marriage is a big deal. At least it should be."

Lara studied her coffee, watching the steam curl over the lip of the cup. "I'm not the best person to comment on that," she admitted. "I got married for all of the wrong reasons, which is precisely why it didn't last."

"Jeffrey Dunham." Finn said the name almost like a curse.

And no wonder. Lara's ex was legendary for his cutting restaurant reviews. Chefs in the five boroughs both feared and loathed him. Her father had been livid when she'd announced their engagement.

"If you go through with this, I no longer have a daughter," he'd warned when he'd stopped by her apartment the morning of her wedding. The ceremony was to be a low-key affair performed at the courthouse.

"That should make you happy," she'd shot back. "I've been such a disappointment to you."

"You've never disappointed me, Lara, until now. You don't love him."

"How do you know? How in the hell do you know anything about me?" she'd shot back defensively. "You've never spent enough time in my presence, unless it was at your restaurant, to know what I think or feel about anything."

"Tell me you love him," Clifton had dared her. "Tell me you're not marrying him to spite me."

"That's just a bonus," she'd snapped, unable to admit to either of them that he was right.

Now, with shame burning her cheeks as she sat across from Finn, she said, "It wasn't my finest moment."

"The guy's an ass. I can say that even though I've never personally been on the receiving end of his abuse. And that's what a lot of his reviews are, in my opinion. They aren't mere criticism. He gets too personal for that."

Lara nodded. "He questioned whether the Chesterfield's famous house dressing came from a bottle at the corner grocery store."

Finn grimaced. "The infamous two-star rating."

"That's how we met. My father was outraged. He sent me to the newspaper to demand a retraction." She pinched her eyes shut and shook her head. "I wound up accepting Jeff's invitation to the opera instead."

"You like opera?"

"I like *Phantom of the Opera*, but the real stuff?" She shook her head. "I went to irritate my dad and then I kept dating Jeff when my dad forbade it. Marriage was my coup de grâce."

"How long did it last?"

"Not long enough to set up proper housekeeping. I came to my senses within a few months. But long enough that my father has barely spoken to me since."

It was none of Finn's business and the answer seemed obvious. Still, he heard himself ask, "Did you love him?"

"No." Lara's regret was plain. "I married him solely to piss off my father. And I did a bang-up job of that. As for Jeff, he didn't love me either. I think he just liked the idea of making my father squirm, which makes our marriage all the more…unforgivable."

"Yet you want forgiveness."

Lara swallowed. "I want a relationship with my father before it's too late, one that isn't filled with acrimony and distrust. The odds for that aren't looking all that good at the moment."

From Finn's perspective, Clifton had wronged Lara as well, but rather than point that out, he opted to change the subject. This one was only serving to make her sad. Already, she was frowning.

"I was wondering if I could ask a favor."

She blinked, but nodded. "I guess so."

"My mom's birthday is coming up. She's turning sixty. My sisters are planning a big family party, and I've been told that I can't cop out and bring flowers this year. I need to buy an actual gift."

"And you want me to help you pick out something special for her?"

"Yeah. So, will you help me?"

"Sure," Lara said. "I guess I can do that."

"Terrific. Thanks."

She rested her elbows on the edge of the table. "Why don't you tell me a little about her? What are her interests, her hobbies?"

He scratched his cheek, thinking. "Well, she likes to cook. In fact, once she heard about the party, she took over the menu and is insisting on making all of the food."

"Is that how you first became interested in the culinary arts?"

"Yeah." He grinned, warmed by the memories. While Lara's father apparently had turned cooking into a chore if not an outright punishment, Finn's mom had made it fun. Helping her prepare meals and make desserts in the family kitchen had been like a reward. For keeping his room clean, she'd shared her double-chocolate-brownies recipe. And when he got straight A's on his report card, she'd taught him how to make the stuffed pork chops his father claimed were the best in the state. "She's a great cook, even if she's not formally trained. A lot of her recipes came from her mother."

Some of those recipes had made it onto his restaurant's menu. A couple, including the one for meat sauce, had made it into the cookbook. Sheryl had laid claim to them all in the divorce.

"She must be really proud of you." Lara didn't quite sigh afterward, but her envy was plain.

Finn took a moment to count his blessings. "She is. Both she and my dad made a lot of sacrifices so they could send me to culinary school."

And they'd made even more sacrifices so he could open his restaurant. Finn took a sip of his coffee, but was unable to wash away the sour taste in his mouth. He felt he'd let them down, even though they had assured him repeatedly that that wasn't the case.

"Does she need anything for her kitchen? A new stand mixer, maybe, or a food processor?"

He shook his head. "I think she has every gadget known to man."

"Hmm. Maybe we should go the noncooking route, then. What are her other interests and hobbies?"

"Well, she likes to garden, but we don't have a lot of yard. Mostly she just grows herbs in pots on the back patio."

"Nothing like fresh herbs," Lara said on a smile. "I have some in a planter on the fire escape. A houseplant, maybe?"

He shook his head. "She already has a veritable jungle indoors. My dad complains it's like living in the tropics."

Lara sipped her coffee. "You said she's turning sixty?"

"That's right."

"Sixty is a milestone birthday. Is there something she's always wanted to do? Or maybe someplace she's always wanted to visit? I don't know what your budget is or if you and your sisters could go in together, but a trip…" She shrugged. "It's just a thought."

Finn smiled. "I should have come to you sooner. My sisters already have their gifts. The same for my dad. If they didn't, I would suggest we all pitch in to send her on a European riverboat cruise. She's always talked about going on one."

"I've seen the television advertisements for those. I'm

not much for structured tours. I'd rather kick around on my own. But they look like they could be a lot of fun, especially for older couples. Maybe you and your sisters could send your folks on one for their anniversary."

"That's a thought," Finn said, filing Lara's suggestion away for later. Then, because he was curious, he asked, "Did you enjoy the time you spent in Europe? I know you were apprenticing, but I assume you had time to get out and see the sights."

"I did. I hit the museums and did some of the touristy things, but mostly I ate." Her expression was satisfied and all the sexier for it. "As much as a country's art and architecture, its food makes a statement about the people who live there."

Finn knew exactly what she meant, so he asked, "Your favorite dish—what was it and where did you eat it?"

Lara didn't hesitate. "Veal scallopini. I ordered it in an Italian restaurant in Paris."

"Italian food in France?" He couldn't help but be skeptical.

"It was very authentic. The owner was from Ceprano originally. He made the scallopini in brown butter and capers." She made a humming sound of satisfaction that had a decidedly disturbing effect on Finn's body.

"That good?"

"I've never had better."

"That sounds like a dare."

Her lips twitched. "Just stating fact."

"I make a mean veal scallopini."

"Really?"

"You doubt me?" he challenged—enjoying himself, enjoying their conversation.

"No. But, you know." She lifted her shoulders along with one of her eyebrows. "Actions speak louder than words."

"I'll cook it for you sometime." Finn didn't make the

offer lightly. He hadn't cooked for a woman since his divorce. Cooking was personal. In his mind, it was every bit as intimate as making love.

"Okay. I'll hold off passing judgment until then."

They studied one another in potent silence. Because he was sorely tempted to lean across the table and kiss her, he said, "Getting back to my mom and a suitable birthday present, what do you think about a necklace?"

Lara pursed her lips. "Does she wear jewelry?"

He mulled the question a moment. "Not really. She has a mother's ring with our birthstones in it, and her wedding ring, of course."

"Then I don't think it's a good idea, especially for an important birthday like sixty. A woman who's turning sixty deserves a gift that recognizes not only what she's accomplished, but what she still wants to do with her life."

Finn snapped his fingers as the idea came to him. "Tap shoes."

"Excuse me?"

"My mom told me once that she took tap lessons when she was a girl, but had to drop out after the first year. Her father got sick and there wasn't any money for nonessentials. She still does this little shuffle-step thing around the house sometimes." He chuckled softly at the memory.

"Then you should get her those shoes and maybe lessons to go along with them. Totally beats a necklace that she isn't likely to wear."

"Yeah, it does." He nodded, both grateful for Lara's help and amazed by how perfectly she seemed to understand him.

Lara offered to go shopping with him. Neither of them had a clue where to look for tap shoes or lessons, but Finn's smartphone solved that dilemma. He punched in some keywords and a moment later he had a list of options. They started with the one closest to Isadora's.

It was within walking distance, and the weather was pleasant if humid. A storm was predicted for later in the day. At the moment, Finn felt one building inside him, especially when his hand accidentally brushed Lara's as they walked. When it did so a second time, he took hold of hers. When their palms met, he felt thunder crash in his chest and lightning streak up from the point of contact.

What kind of heel did it make him, Finn wondered, that he was glad they were no longer competing against one another?

It took three stops before they found what they were looking for: a studio that had beginner classes specifically aimed at adults. The bonus was that particular business operated a second studio in Queens not far from his parents' duplex. Since he was uncertain what size his mother wore, Finn took a picture of a pair of tap shoes with his phone. Lara suggested he have the photo made into a card and tuck the gift certificate he'd purchased for lessons inside.

All in all, he was pleased with himself. And he was grateful to Lara.

"Going to your parents' for dinner tonight?" she asked.

"Not tonight."

"You're not working, are you?"

"No. I cleared my schedule for the next several weeks to accommodate the competition."

"Several?" she asked drily.

He offered a lopsided grin. "What can I say? I'm feeling optimistic."

"I hope you win." Her tone had turned serious. "I...I've been thinking about this. I wanted that job. I wanted a fresh start with my father, and I wanted to show him what I can do. But if it can't be me running the Chesterfield's kitchen... Well, I'd rather it be you than anyone else."

"Thank you," Finn replied. "That means a lot to me."

This time he didn't wait for their hands to brush as they walked. He took hers and held it as a feeling of rightness settled over him. For the first time in a long time, everything was going Finn's way.

CHAPTER NINE

Let simmer

THEY HADN'T MADE plans before parting the day before, but Finn woke just before eight the next morning without the aid of an alarm clock—a major feat for someone used to sleeping in—eager to call Lara. He waited until nine, figuring she would be up and hopefully back from Isadora's by then, assuming she had gone for coffee.

She answered on the third ring, sounding a little breathless.

"Hey, Lara. It's Finn. Am I catching you at a bad time?"

"Just…finishing up…a workout," she managed to get out between breaths.

His mind went into fantasy mode, picturing her wearing something tight and skimpy, skin aglow with the sheen of perspiration. He just barely held back a moan.

"I can call back."

"Give me…fifteen…'kay?"

"You've got it." He figured it was going to take at least that long to get his own pulse under control.

His heart was still pumping a bit irregularly when he redialed her number. This time when Lara answered, she didn't sound winded, but that didn't prevent him from picturing her wearing curve-hugging Lycra.

"What's up?" she asked.

Finn glanced at his lap, but decided not to state the obvious. "I know it's last-minute, but I was wondering if you have plans this evening."

"No. Well, not unless you count rearranging the furniture in my apartment." Her tone was rueful.

"Is this a regularly scheduled event?" he asked with a grin as he settled back on the couch and propped his feet up on the coffee table.

"It is when I'm having a bad week. I've done it twice already," she admitted. "Last night I got up to get a glass of water and stubbed my big toe on an end table."

"Sounds hazardous."

"Very." But she was laughing.

"When I'm having a bad week, I uncap a beer and watch ESPN," Finn replied, his gaze on the flat screen that was mounted on the living room's opposite wall.

She laughed again, as he'd hoped she would. He liked knowing he could tease her out of a bad mood, even if only briefly. He wasn't kidding himself. Lara's strained ties to her father were well beyond Finn's ability to fix. Indeed, they were beyond his ability to fathom, given how close he was to his parents.

She was saying, "So, why do you ask? Do you need more help shopping for gifts, or perhaps you're considering another kite-flying adventure?"

"No shopping. I try to limit myself to once in a blue moon. As for kite-flying, it's supposed to storm later, and as much as I enjoyed our outing in the park the other day, I'm not interested in pulling a Ben Franklin."

More laughter flowed through the phone line before she asked, "So, what do you want to do?"

It was an innocuous question that inspired a primal response. He cleared his throat as he attempted to clear his mind of inappropriate thoughts. "I've got two tickets to a

Broadway musical. The network gave them to all of us as a way to apologize for the inconvenience of this week."

He winced upon saying it. Way to make her feel better.

But Lara didn't sound offended when she replied, "Well, then, it's only fair you take me, seeing as how I provided the inconvenience in question. What's playing?"

"Annie."

"And you want to go see it?" She sounded doubtful.

He couldn't blame her. The family-friendly musical about a spunky orphan wasn't high on his list of must-see productions. But…

"I want to go see it with you," he replied truthfully.

It was three painfully long heartbeats before she replied. Finn knew because he counted them.

"All right. But I have one condition."

"What's that?" he asked, ready to agree to almost anything.

"You'll let me make you dinner beforehand."

It seemed like a fair trade to Lara and an opportunity to show off her skills in an atmosphere that might not be competitive, but definitely counted. What Finn thought of her ability in the kitchen mattered. It mattered a lot.

So, she found herself going to three of her favorite markets before noon, on the hunt for the perfect green beans, the freshest salmon and the ripest melons to create the meal she had in mind. Finn had insisted on bringing wine, so that was taken care of. As for rolls, since she didn't have time to make them from scratch as she would have preferred, she stopped at a bakery not far from her apartment and picked up half a dozen hard-crusted baguettes.

Meal preparations were well under way, and she had showered, dressed, applied makeup and managed to do something with her hair by the time the buzzer announced his arrival at five o'clock.

She was waiting at the door when he came up the stairs. He stopped at the landing with half a flight to go, his smile as slow and deliberate as his gaze while he took in her attire.

Lara had gone with a skirt and silk top. She didn't wear a skirt often. When styling food, she preferred to wear pants, since she sometimes found herself kneeling or crouching to survey a shot from all possible angles. But she liked getting dressed up every now and then, and putting on high heels. Her legs, which were slender at the ankle and curved at the calf from rigorous workouts, were one of her better features, or so she'd been told. Finn's approving grin made it plain that he concurred.

"Don't you clean up nicely, Ms. Dunham," he drawled when he reached the top of the stairs.

"I was thinking the same thing," Lara replied.

He'd tamed his hair and shaved off the stubble that she'd found sexy. But she had no complaints. Wearing dark slacks and a crisp white button-down shirt that he'd left open at the throat, he looked every bit as delicious as the melon sorbet she'd prepared for dessert.

He handed her the wine and then took her face between his hands. He leaned in for a kiss that had her toes trying to curl inside the narrow points of her pumps.

Afterward she asked breathlessly, "What was that for?"

"I wanted to thank you for dinner."

Still feeling a little dazed, she said, "We haven't eaten yet."

"Just getting it out of the way." He grinned and she felt her heart rate spike.

Inside her apartment, Finn sniffed the air. "It smells like heaven in here."

"Thank you."

"Tarragon?" he asked.

She nodded and waited, knowing that, as a chef, he would want to identify the spices himself.

"Dill."

"Yes."

"Lemon and garlic."

"Uh-huh."

"You made salmon."

"Herb-crusted with blanched green beans drizzled with lemon and olive oil and a pinch of sea salt."

He made the appropriate sounds of appreciation in return.

They'd walked while they talked, so they were now in her kitchen. It was smaller than she would have liked, but actually quite large by New York real-estate standards. Still, the room had all of the essentials for a chef, including a six-burner gas stove, a decent amount of prep space and a French door refrigerator that could hold more perishable food than Lara could eat in a month.

Because she loved to cook for more than just herself, and considered it a sin to throw out the fruits of her labor, she'd gotten to know several of her neighbors and routinely dropped off meals to them. Dana, of course, was a regular, too.

"Nice," Finn said.

"Thanks. It was the only room in the apartment I remodeled after I bought the place a couple of years ago." Her tone turned wry. "The bathroom is still a disaster with this really ugly green-and-orange tile, but this was my priority."

"I can understand that." He smiled, nodded. "So, do you want me to open the wine?"

"Yes, thanks. The corkscrew is in the top drawer on the far left, and I have an aerator in the cabinet just above that along with wineglasses."

While Finn got to work on that, Lara started plating. Her apartment was too small for a separate dining room, and when she'd enlarged the kitchen, she'd used any space that might have allowed for a table. As a result, whenever she had company for dinner, they ate at the small bar area that was mounted flush against the far wall. Since she didn't entertain often, she'd had to clear off the stack of magazines and cookbooks to make room for her and Finn.

When it came to setting the scene, she preferred a real table, but she'd made that meager strip of butcher block look pretty good, if she did say so herself. While out shopping, she'd picked up some blue hydrangea, and she'd arranged the fat blooms with some greenery in a squat, square vase. On either side of the arrangement, she'd placed white taper candles in delicate glass holders.

With the food plated, she set it on a pair of blue-and-white-checked place mats that gave off a French country vibe. White cloth napkins finished the look.

"You do know what you're doing," Finn said, coming up beside her. He handed her a glass of wine.

After taking a sip, she told him, "I could say the same for you when it comes to picking out wine."

The full-bodied wine would hold up nicely against the salmon.

"You said red and this is my favorite."

"Mine, too, now. I'm catching a hint of vanilla and oak," she said.

He nodded. "It was aged in oak barrels."

"French or American?" she asked. In wine circles there continued to be a raging debate over which country had the best.

Finn apparently knew this, because he grinned and neatly sidestepped the issue. "I'll never tell."

She set her wine on the place mat. "Have a seat. I'll be right back."

While Finn settled on one of the backless stools at the bar, she turned down the kitchen light, which was on a dimmer switch. Then she picked up the remote control and hit play. Miles Davis's trumpet wailed from the speakers for a brief moment before she lowered the volume to a level more conducive to conversation.

"A jazz fan?" Finn asked when she joined him at the bar.

"Since my first year of culinary school," she replied. "I dated a moody guy who loved Coltrane, smoked clove cigarettes and drank bourbon. I never acquired a taste for hard liquor or cigarettes of any variety, thank God. And the relationship only lasted half a semester, but I was hooked on jazz. If you'd prefer another genre of music, I can change it."

"No. I don't listen to jazz often, but I don't mind it." He regarded her for a moment and then picked up his glass. "I feel like I should propose a toast before we begin eating."

"All right." She wrapped her fingers around the thin stem of her glass and lifted it halfway to her lips.

"To happy beginnings." He smiled and clinked the rim of his goblet against the side of hers.

It was an interesting toast, one that conveniently overlooked the fact that Lara had recently suffered both a personal and professional setback. Yet, she agreed with Finn. In spite of everything, this was a happy beginning.

Finn wasn't a fan of musical theater, especially productions that included spunky children belting out catchy show tunes that he'd bet his bottom dollar he would be singing in his head for a good week to come. That said, he enjoyed *Annie*. A lot.

In fact, he was sorry to see the curtain come down, because unless Lara agreed to go someplace and have a drink with him, it meant their evening out was drawing to a close.

The feelings she'd inspired in such a short time were crazy. They scared the hell out of him. Once burned, twice shy and all that. Scared or not, he couldn't stay away.

A little while later, they followed the crowd as it spilled outside onto the street. Then they walked aimlessly for a couple of blocks, making their way to Times Square.

"It's getting late," she said.

"Too late for a drink?"

She turned, smiled. "No. It's not like I have to get up early."

He nodded. Neither of them had to be up early. They could sleep as late as they wanted…assuming they slept at all.

But he was getting ahead of himself.

After clearing his throat, he said, "I know a place not far from where we first met that has a decent wine list. It also serves amazing appetizers."

"Sounds good. Is that where you were coming from when you stepped out to hail the cab?"

"Actually, I was coming from my apartment. I have a studio not far from there."

Her steps slowed, but she was grinning when she asked, "Is this place that serves the amazing appetizers yours, by any chance?"

"No. It's a real pub. Spanky's. Ever been?"

Finn wasn't sure if she looked relieved or disappointed that they weren't heading to his apartment, although he knew which category he fell into.

"No. But I've passed by it several times on my way to the magazine for styling jobs."

It didn't take long to get to Spanky's. Even though it was a weeknight, it was relatively busy. The after-work crowd of suited professionals had long since moved on. The people seated at the tables and along the bar were mostly college-aged with a few saltier old-timers thrown in.

"Nice place. Comfortable," Lara said as they wound their way through high-top tables to a booth in the back.

"Yeah. I think so, too."

No big-screen televisions were mounted on the walls, tuned to sporting events. No kitschy flea-market finds hung from the ceiling. The decor leaned rustic—not so much mountain cabin as family lake cottage. Specifically, *his* family's cottage on a small lake in Vermont. The theme should have been an odd fit for Manhattan. In fact, a couple of bank loan officers had warned against it, but his cousin Joanna, the proprietress, had held firm and scraped together her start-up money despite their predictions. Spanky's hadn't hurt for customers since its weathered doors had opened the spring before last.

Finn credited his cousin's vision for that. Spanky's was the sort of place where people could gather and relax while tossing back a cold one, whether that beer was microbrewed or imported, or sip a quality glass of Chardonnay without overpaying. Add in good, reasonably priced food and word had gotten around quickly.

"I think the woman standing behind the bar is trying to get your attention," Lara remarked.

He didn't need to look over to figure out whom she meant. At this time of night, Joanna would be at the tap. And the fact that Finn was there with a woman would have sent his cousin's curiosity into overdrive.

"Try to ignore her. I do."

"I take it she's a friend of yours."

"More like family. She's my cousin. And she owns this place."

"She's Spanky?" Lara's lips twitched with a smile that went on to dance in her eyes.

"A nickname from childhood."

"Let me guess," Lara said drily. "You gave it to her."

He spread his hands wide and shrugged. "What are cousins for?"

"Hmm, I'm guessing if that cousin also is a talented chef, he helped put together a menu."

He nodded. "Spanky's may be more bar than restaurant, but Joanna didn't want to serve the standard pub food, so when she opened, I offered a few suggestions."

"That was nice of you," Lara said.

He shrugged. "We're family."

"Not all families are like yours."

Lara's specifically. He swallowed an apology he knew would only make her uncomfortable.

"Now that I know you had a hand in the menu, I'm eager to sample those appetizers you mentioned earlier."

"You won't be disappointed."

Lara merely smiled at the boast.

Rather than sending one of her waitstaff, Joanna came over to take their orders. Finn had expected as much. Since the dust had settled on his divorce, all of the women in his family had been doing their damnedest to set him up on a date. He had little doubt that news he'd been spotted out with a woman would make it through the Westbrook grapevine before he paid the check.

No sense throwing kerosene on a fire that posed the threat of raging out of control all on its own. So, as soon as he saw her heading in their direction, he said to Lara, "I'm going to warn you, the women in my family are notoriously nosy. She's going to try to pump you for information. Reply with one-word answers."

"And if she threatens to march me into the back room and break out the truth serum?"

"Go ahead and laugh," Finn said, having a hard time not doing so himself. Managing to keep his tone dire, he added, "Don't complain later that you weren't warned."

"No complaining. Got it." Lara executed a jaunty salute just as his cousin reached the table.

Joanna was five years Finn's junior. She was tall for a woman at just a hair under six feet. As kids, he had been able to hoist her over one shoulder without much effort and lock her in the creepy cellar at their grandparents' house. These days no one got the upper hand on Joanna, which was why he didn't worry about her working a bar in the city late at night.

"Hello, Finn," she said, drawing even with their table. "I didn't know you were coming in this evening or that you'd be bringing a...*friend*." She bobbed her eyebrows.

Subtle. The word wasn't in her vocabulary, or the vocabulary of any of the women in his family, for that matter.

"It was a last-minute thing. Lara and I were out not far from here and..." He shrugged and left it at that, knowing full well Joanna would fill in the blanks for herself.

"Well, you know I'm always happy to see you." Joanna smiled before adding meaningfully, "And it's great to see you out with a...*friend*."

It was all Finn could do to hold back a groan.

"Are you going to introduce us?" his cousin asked.

"Joanna, Lara." He made a sweeping motion between them.

"It's nice to meet you." Lara offered her hand.

"Same here."

"I like your place. It's very comfortable."

"Thank you. That's exactly what I was going for." Joanna's gaze swung to Finn. "I like her."

"That makes two of us," he said.

"What can I get for you?" she asked Lara.

Lara tucked the wine list back into its spot amid the condiments on the tabletop. "I'd like a glass of the house red, please."

"Coming right up." To Finn she said, "Your usual beer?"

He nodded. "And a plate of the asparagus."

"Asparagus?" Lara asked.

"It's wrapped in prosciutto and flaky pastry dough," he told her.

"It's excellent. Customers rave about it all the time," Joanna offered as a testimonial.

"Lara will be the judge. She's a chef."

"No kidding?" His cousin's eyes rounded. "I never thought you'd hook up with another one of those."

That statement had Lara's eyebrows rising.

While Finn hoped his cousin would retreat to the bar, she rattled on, peppering Lara with questions.

"Are you a private chef like Finn? Did you meet through work? Oh, my God, you're not in that competition he's doing at the Cuisine Cable Network, are you?" She took a breath, sighed. "Star-crossed chefs."

"Lara's not on the show," Finn said. If only he'd stopped there, but the word *anymore* slipped out.

"Oh? Oh, no! You've already been eliminated. Gosh, I am so sorry."

The light in Spanky's was low, but Finn was able to see color flood into Lara's cheeks.

"Jo—"

But his cousin was on a roll. "That's a real bummer, but hey, better luck next time, right? You've got to keep at it. I mean, look at Finn here. He's had some hard knocks, too. That's life. It's taken some time, but he's picked himself up, dusted himself off and now he's *finally* back in the game." Joanna cleared her throat. "Um, not that dating is a game, but, well, you know what I mean."

"Yeah, we know," Finn said drily. "Can we get our drinks now?"

"Sure." Joanna pulled a face. "Listen to me, going on and on.... Just for that, your first round will be on the house."

"What happened to one-syllable answers," Lara murmured as his cousin walked away.

Finn laughed. "Sorry about that."

"That's all right," Lara replied. "Actually, she answered a question for me."

"What might that be?"

"How often you get out. From her barely contained excitement over your bringing in a *friend*, you're obviously not much of a player."

He chuckled drily. "I've never been much of a player. But, um, I haven't been involved with anyone for a while."

After that, they made small talk until their drinks arrived. A group of tourists came in, keeping Joanna busy behind the bar, so a waitress delivered their beverages.

"Your appetizer will be up in a minute," the young woman assured them before leaving.

Lara sipped her wine, savoring it in a way that made Finn want to groan.

"This is very good. It would pair well with this veal dish I make."

"What's in it?"

She described a dish that had his mouth starting to water not only because of the ingredients, but because of the woman he envisioned working with them.

"You'll have to make it for me next time. Or you can show me how to make it."

She nodded, seeming not the least bit surprised that he was already planning another dinner date with her.

"I'd like that."

Lara eyed her nearly empty glass. The merlot had left her feeling warm and relaxed. The man sitting across from her had helped even more. Finn was a welcome respite from her current reality.

No, not a respite. That diminished his importance in her life. He was a bright spot, a highlight. He was the unexpected, but breathtaking rainbow after a particularly vicious storm.

"You're smiling," he said.

"Yeah." Her lips bowed further. "I am. Thank you."

"For?"

"Just...thank you," she replied, feeling embarrassed.

"I think I know what you mean."

"Yeah?"

"Yeah." He nodded. "Right back at you."

When the waitress arrived with their appetizer, Lara ordered another glass of wine and told him, "If you'd like a second beer, this round is on me."

"All right." He nodded to the waitress.

"These look good," Lara told him as she picked up one of the prosciutto-wrapped asparagus spears. The flaky pastry that spiraled around it was baked a light golden-brown.

"So says the food stylist. I'm more interested in how you think they taste."

His ribbing was good-natured, so she wasn't offended. Still, she made a tsking sound before reminding him in a haughty tone, "First and foremost, food is a visual experience. We see a dish and we smell it, before we finally taste it. For a truly satisfying experience, you have to use more than one sense."

He leaned over and took a bite of the appetizer she held. A sexy smile appeared afterward when he added, "Eating is not the only activity I can think of that uses a few of our senses for a truly satisfying experience."

Sparks shot up Lara's spine along with the first licks of excitement. She sampled what remained of the appetizer in her hand.

"Well?" he asked afterward. "What do you think?"

"It was every bit as good as you promised it would be."

Maybe even better since the man responsible for the recipe was so damned tantalizing.

Her mouth watered when he smiled and said, "It makes an excellent first course."

She pretended to mull that over before asking, "Care to tell me what you would make for the main dish?"

Lara swore the temperature in the bar spiked by several degrees when Finn replied, "I'd rather show you."

CHAPTER TEN

Bring to a boil

IMPULSIVENESS HAD COST Lara big in the past, so she tended to skate on the edge of the pond, rather than venturing out where the ice might not be thick enough to hold her. Since her hasty marriage and equally hasty divorce, she'd taken things slowly when it came to men. She'd been on a lot of first dates that never led to a second. Mostly that was her choice, and it explained why it had been so long since she'd had sex.

Better to be safe than satisfied and sorry. That was her motto.

But tonight? With Finn?

Everything seemed different and full of promise, even if the rest of her life was in the proverbial crapper.

It was closing in on eleven o'clock when they finished their second round of drinks. The appetizer was long gone by then, polished off handily between the pair of them. Finn paid the tab. He refused her offer to cover the second round of drinks, although he reluctantly agreed to let her leave the tip. Lara was used to paying her own way. Maybe it was foolish, but it made her feel in control. A decision-maker rather than a blind participant.

Outside, the evening was hot and humid. The air was heavy with the mingling scents of exhaust fumes and ripe produce from a fruit market a couple of doors down. She expected Finn to hail a cab. Instead, he took her hand and started walking. A moment later, they passed the building where she'd styled the food for the magazine photo shoot. Had that been only a week ago?

Just beyond it, he stopped and fished a key ring out of his pocket. The nondescript door he unlocked was wedged between two shop windows.

"You live…here?"

"Yeah." His laughter sounded self-conscious. "I know it doesn't look like it from the street, but upstairs the former commercial space has been divided up into a handful of decent apartments."

Once inside, they followed a long hall that led to what appeared to be a freight elevator. Its doors were metal, adorned with graffiti and opened horizontally. After they closed, he used his key again, pushed a button, and when the lift stopped half a dozen floors up, the doors opened to a spacious studio apartment with exposed ductwork, a worn wooden plank floor and redbrick walls. But what caught her attention was the kitchen.

"Oh, my God! I am so jealous," she said, kicking off her heels and crossing to it. The floor was poured concrete and cold under her bare feet. "Your island is bigger than my entire kitchen, even after I demoed a wall to make room for my six-burner."

He was grinning. Gone was any self-consciousness. "The amount of space was what sold me on the place."

"How did you stumble on this?"

"I have a cousin who's a developer."

Lara turned and took in the rest of the room. Despite the high ceilings and overall industrial vibe from the architecture, the room was surprisingly inviting. The tall windows helped. During the day, they would allow in a generous amount of light. They were bracketed in gauzy white floor-to-ceiling curtains. Even though the view wasn't the greatest—no skyline was visible, just the facades of other buildings—it still helped keep the place airy.

"Nice curtains."

"My sisters' doing. They claimed the place echoed."

Family again. The man's life was full of kin willing to rush in and lend a hand. It was impossible not to envy him for that.

Finn cleared his throat and the sound bounced off the ceiling to boomerang back, causing Lara to laugh.

"Okay, they may have had a point," he added drily.

"Have you lived here long?"

Other than the kitchen, it was sparsely furnished, so it came as a surprise when he replied, "A couple years. I haven't gotten around to furnishing it."

That was an understatement. The room sported a sofa, large-screen television, of course, a packing crate that served as an end table and not much else. She didn't even see a proper bed, leaving her to assume he either slept on the couch or it pulled out to reveal a mattress.

That might not be odd for a recent college graduate, but Finn was in his mid-thirties.

"Can I ask you something?"

"Sure," he said.

This time it was the sound of Lara clearing her throat that echoed in the cavernous room. "How long have you been divorced?"

"That obvious?" He rubbed the back of his neck.

She shrugged. "My apartment was pretty sparse for a while after I left Jeffrey. I didn't mind that he kept the sectional sofa or the bedroom set. But I was pretty pissed when he laid claim to the food processor."

"Bastard."

She chuckled at Finn's dry delivery before admitting, "I

smuggled his golf clubs out of our storage locker and held them hostage until he agreed to hand it over."

"Clever. Remind me never to get on your bad side."

"Well?"

He glanced around. "It's been a couple of years since we split. My ex and my lawyer made out like bandits."

She made an appropriately sympathetic sound before telling Finn, "It's been nearly six for me."

Lara had done a lot of growing up since then, and even more soul-searching. While she still couldn't say she was ready to dive back into a serious commitment, neither did she want to get involved, even on the most casual basis, with someone who was still pining for someone else.

From his overall demeanor, Finn didn't appear to be in love with his ex, but it wouldn't hurt to ask a few more questions, she reasoned. Get the lay of the land, so to speak, before deciding whether or not she wanted to pitch a tent.

"How long were you married?"

"Five years. Sheryl opted for an early-out clause two days after our anniversary. It wasn't a huge surprise. I knew something was wrong. I'd been after her to go with me to counseling."

He'd wanted to save his marriage, which was commendable. In Lara's case, there had been nothing to save. "Do you have any kids?"

"None." Finn scrubbed a hand over his chin. "Even before things started to head south, we'd agreed to wait to start a family. That wound up being a good thing. The split was ugly enough without a custody dispute."

No kids meant no permanent ties to his ex. That was another plus in Lara's book. She never had to see Jeffrey again, and that suited her just fine. Still, she wrinkled her nose and offered a heartfelt "Sorry."

"I was, too, at the time." His laughter was rueful, and carried a dash of bitterness when he added, "I got over it pretty quickly when I learned that she was sleeping with my best friend and silent business partner. Former best friend and former business partner now."

"Ouch."

"That didn't bother me as much as the fact that she took my restaurant and laid claim to all of my recipes."

Lara blinked before her eyes rounded. How was it possible, she wondered, that she hadn't put two and two together until just then?

"You're *Griffin* Westbrook!"

At one time, he'd been the next big thing on New York's culinary scene with a restaurant in the theater district that was almost as well-known as the Chesterfield. Then he'd lost everything in a very nasty, very public divorce.

She was vague on the particulars, but she recalled some sort of dispute regarding who had come up with the restaurant's signature dishes.

"Guilty as charged," he said. "For the record, only my mother, my ex's lawyer and the media refer to me as *Griffin.*"

Lara found herself apologizing again. "Sorry. That was rude."

But Finn shrugged. "My life's an open book."

His words shook loose another recollection. "Didn't the two of you write a cookbook together?"

He nodded. "Actually, I was the creative force behind it." He coughed for effect and plucked at the front of his shirt when he added, "Which, by the way, went on to be nominated for a James Beard award."

"I remember. Impressive."

"What else do you remember?" he asked.

Before she could think better of it, she said, "There was some sort of scan…"

"Scandal," he finished for her.

"We don't have to talk about it."

"I don't mind. It's ancient history." But the muscle that ticked in his jaw told her otherwise. He might not be mooning over his ex, but he was still smarting from betrayal. "Romantic that I was, I dedicated the book to Sheryl. Her high-priced lawyer twisted my words about owing her 'everything' around to imply that she'd been the creative force behind it. And since she'd been the one to make the rounds to publicize the book—media interviews, personal appearances, book signings—while I held down the fort at the restaurant—they used that, too, as 'proof' that Sheryl was the actual author."

"Wow."

"Yeah. It was brutal. My reputation took a huge hit."

Which explained why he was so desperate to win the competition and restore his name in the court of public opinion. But she decided to lighten the mood.

"It's pretty rare I meet anyone as infamous in New York culinary circles as I am."

He laughed, as she'd hoped he would. She liked the sound, not to mention the way Finn looked with his head tipped back and his lips curved up.

"If it makes you feel any better, my ex gave your former restaurant a terrible review in last week's column," she told him. "I didn't read the actual article, but the headline included the word *inedible* to describe the braised veal."

"Yeah, I saw that. I'd like to be happy that she's running Rascal's into the ground, but…"

His smile ebbed as his words trailed away.

Lara decided to change the subject. She wasn't really hungry, but, taking a seat on one of the stools at the island, she said, "At Spanky's you mentioned something about a main course."

"Right. I did." Instead of reaching for Lara, however, he turned toward the fridge. "It's been a while since I went shopping, so what I make depends on what I have in here."

He opened both stainless-steel doors and stood with his back to her. While he perused the shelves, she perused his physique. Just as she'd told Dana, he was certified prime from the broad shoulders beneath his dress shirt right down to the firm butt that filled out his pants.

"How hungry are you?"

Gaze still on his butt, she murmured without thinking, "Famished."

He turned and she felt her cheeks heat. A look passed between them. His expression was pure male. She'd seen several versions of it so far. When they'd first met and brushed hands by the cab. When they'd gone for coffee after she was outed as Clifton's daughter and ousted from the show. While flying a kite in Central Park. And earlier that very evening at Spanky's, when they'd discussed appetizers as a prelude to main dishes. All of those looks had been potent, but this one...this one could have started an out-of-control brushfire in a downpour.

"I have some fresh pasta and the fixings for a simple Bolognese, but, as you know, to do the sauce right, it takes time. The flavors need to mature."

"And meld together," she agreed on a nod.

"How patient are you feeling, Lara?"

Now, there was a question.

"Not very. Patience hasn't gotten me very far lately."

"So, I was thinking..." He took a covered bowl out of the fridge and closed the doors. "I have these leftovers from yesterday's dinner. Thai chicken."

Was he just teasing her now? She couldn't be sure.

"It sounds spicy."

"It is. Very." His gaze flicked briefly to her mouth. "Interested?"

"Very," she repeated. She wasn't talking about the chicken, and the heat glowing in his eyes confirmed that he wasn't either. Thank heavens! "Can I sample a little?"

"Sure. Want me to warm it up?"

Lara shook her head as she came around the island. "That's all right."

He opened the bowl, but that was as far as he got before they reached for each other. Distantly, she was aware of the scents of ginger, cilantro and sriracha sauce. But what filled her senses was Finn. His scent. His touch. His taste.

She couldn't get enough of him. Nor could she get close enough, even though she was plastered against him from thigh to lips. He was warm, firm, welcoming. A sigh escaped. He answered with a moan.

"I've been…thinking about…you and me and…*this*… for a while." As he spoke he nipped his way down to her collarbone.

"Since Spanky's?" she asked, fighting a shiver.

"Before then."

Lara did tremble now as she admitted, "Me, too."

"Yeah?"

"Yeah. Like since *hello*."

He laughed. "Great minds. What else have you been thinking?"

Finn was letting her set the parameters. Even though she'd already made it pretty clear what she wanted, he was leaving her an out, giving her a chance to change her mind. She could pull back and put on the brakes. No harm. No foul. Or she could plow full steam ahead.

Lara didn't feel reckless when she chose the latter. Rather, she felt right.

"Your shirt. I've been wondering what you would look like without it."

Deep laughter rumbled again. With his body still pressed against hers, she felt his mirth as much as she heard it. The sensation was oddly erotic, but what had the breath backing up in her lungs was his reply.

"I've been wondering the same thing. What do you say we both satisfy our curiosity?"

It sounded like a good idea to her. She reached for the top button on her blouse only to have him push her hands away.

"Let me do that."

"Okay, but only if I get to do the same," she replied boldly.

Hunger of a different kind gnawed inside her when Finn got to work unfastening her top. Two buttons in, he stopped to pull the hem from the waistband of her skirt. Fingers skimmed briefly over her waist, a featherlight touch that had her moaning and wanting to demand more. His eyes remained on hers, the corners of his mouth turned up slightly when she trembled. With the last button freed from its hole, he parted the fabric and gave a low whistle.

When he would have pushed the fabric down her sleeves, she stopped him. Lara wasn't overly modest, but some things were best done in private.

"Um, the windows." She gave a nod in their direction. "I kind of feel on display. Would you mind?"

"Be right back."

He left her to yank the gauzy material closed. He also flicked off the lamp, leaving only the under-counter lighting on. The effect made the place feel cocoonlike.

"Where were we?" he asked, even though his smile said he knew.

"Right…about…here." She pushed the fabric apart and over her shoulders, letting it slide down her arms.

He groaned in appreciation, even as Lara grinned.

"And now it's my turn."

CHAPTER ELEVEN

Whisk

IT WAS NEARLY midnight when something roused Finn from sleep. Not something, he realized, coming fully awake. Someone. Lara was up. He could just make out her shadowy form stumbling around in his dark apartment.

Levering up on one elbow, he said, "You can turn on the light, you know."

"That's okay. I'm good."

Her claim was followed by a thud and muted oath. He was pretty sure she'd just banged her kneecap on his makeshift end table. Since Finn had to grab the lamp to keep it from crashing to the floor, he also turned it on.

"Are you all right?"

"Fine."

That made one of them. Finn's heart thunked out an extra beat at the sight of her carelessly wrapped in the throw she'd pulled off the back of his couch. The undergarments he'd helped her remove were clutched in one hand. Her other was holding the blanket in place. His gaze took in the pair of toned legs that had wrapped tightly around his waist at the moment of climax, and the silky hair that was a sexy mess thanks to the hands he'd fisted there, holding tight when passion took him over the edge.

"Sorry. I was trying not to wake you."

"That's all right. And I'm the one who should be apologizing. I didn't mean to fall asleep."

One of the last things Finn remembered before drifting off was collapsing beside her on the sofa bed after some of the most vigorous and inventive lovemaking of his life. If sex were a competitive sport, he was pretty sure they would have brought home the gold.

She chuckled. "I know what you mean. I'm shocked we didn't put each other in a coma."

"Are you…leaving?"

He was surprised to find he didn't want her to go. Since his divorce, the few times he'd invited a woman into his apartment, he'd not had a problem watching them go home afterward. But Lara? He blamed the amazing sex. Surely it was too soon for it to be anything else.

"Yes. I called a cab to come get me. I was just looking for my clothes. I found…a couple of things."

She held up one hand, shook the contents pom-pom style. In it were the two articles of clothing Finn had removed last. He bit back a groan and felt himself grow hard recalling the care he'd taken unhooking her bra and then working the panties down her toned thighs. The unhurried pace of their foreplay had seemed excruciating at the time, but there was no arguing with the end results.

"I'll never get out of here if you keep looking at me like that," she told him.

"Like what?" But he grinned, because he had a pretty good idea what she meant.

"Finn," she said in exasperation. "Make yourself useful."

"Happy to." And certain parts of his anatomy were happier than others to oblige.

"I mean help me look for my clothes," she replied, her tone dry.

"Okay. On one condition."

She eyed him suspiciously. "What might that be?"

"That I get to help you put them back on."

"That's a first," she replied. "I've never had a man offer to dress me before."

"It's a first for me, too. I've never offered."

He wasn't sure why he had now. In fact, watching her stand there clutching the ends of his brown chenille throw together between her breasts to conceal her amazing body, Finn was beginning to think he needed to have his head examined.

Still, dressing her seemed improbably appealing. Foreplay, but in reverse. Which meant it was going to lead to a lot of frustration, but also ratchet up the tension for the next time they were together.

There would be another time. He would make certain of that.

He tossed back the sheet and stood. The fact he was naked didn't make him uncomfortable. And as far as he was concerned, it was a bonus that Lara's gaze detoured south and she began to nibble her bottom lip. While he grabbed his shorts from atop the lampshade where they'd landed earlier, he was aware of her watching him.

"Second thoughts about staying a little longer?" he inquired, slowly pulling the boxers up his legs.

"And third and fourth," she admitted. "But my cab will be here any minute, and I do need to get home."

He nearly asked her why. What was so important that she needed to rush home at this hour? She was unattached, over the age of consent. Like him, she'd been married and was now divorced. She had him on being disowned. Finn had come to accept there was nothing he could do to make his family cut the cord.

Family.

With an inaudible groan he remembered the text he'd received from his younger sister Kristy as he and Lara had left Spanky's. As predicted, the grapevine was in full swing. Kristy had already known all about his date, which meant that his other sister did as well, and probably his mother and an assortment of aunts and cousins.

I'll be in the city tomorrow. Kate, too, the message read, referencing their other sister. We want to talk about Mom's party. Make something spectacular for brunch, please.

He wasn't fooled. They might start with their mother's birthday, but the conversation would drift to his social life soon after. And, even though they'd invited themselves for brunch, they could arrive anytime after dawn. That was just how they operated. His sisters could be obnoxiously nosy and overbearing, but in an endearing way, since they always had his best interests at heart.

Still, Finn didn't want Lara there when they arrived. If his cousin Joanna was on her game, she'd already filled them in on the fact that Lara was a chef and Finn had met her on *Executive Chef Challenge*. And if Lara were still in his apartment... Well, it would be awkward on multiple levels.

He headed to the kitchen.

"I think your top is on the floor in front of the fridge."

Sure enough, it was in a heap next to his shirt, her skirt and his pants. After shedding those articles of clothing, he and Lara had worked their way to the other side of his apartment, where the surfaces were softer and more accommodating to horizontal activity. He picked up the top and, before holding it out, gave it a good shake. Finn kept a tidy kitchen. Organization and neatness were the marks of a good chef. As a result, the countertops were generally free of spills, crumbs and clutter. But he couldn't say the same for his floors.

When Lara tried to take it, he slanted her a look. "Remember our deal. And it applies to your undergarments, too." He was the one who held out a hand this time.

She may have rolled her eyes, but he caught the gleam

of excitement in them. She was game, every bit as eager and interested as he was.

"I never actually agreed to let you dress me," she said. But she placed the items in his hand anyway.

"The blanket." He motioned to it with his chin. "It's in the way."

"So it is."

Very slowly, in a move reminiscent of the way he'd stripped her mere hours earlier, she opened the sides, exposing the soft, gently mounded flesh beneath.

Finn swallowed. It was like Christmas and she was a gift.

"Are you sure you can handle it?" she asked in a husky whisper. "It's harder than it looks."

"How would you know?" he challenged with a meaningful glance south. His boxers were getting tighter by the second.

She chuckled. "I'm talking about putting on a bra. It's an acquired skill, and not as easy as taking one off."

"I think I can manage."

He dropped her top on the counter and stepped closer. Taking the bra from her hand, he used both of his to hold it out chest high in front of her.

"Slip your arms through the straps. That's it," he murmured, stepping forward and regrettably closing the gap between silk and what he considered perfection.

"Well?" she prodded when he just stood there. "Are you going to fasten it or what?"

The *or what* was an enticing proposition. On a groan he finished the task, silently congratulating himself until he realized that her panties would be next. He'd made it over one hurdle only to be confronted by another, much higher one.

He hooked their waistband over the tip of his index finger and gave them a twirl while he contemplated a strategy. Every scenario he could think of required bending and would bring him into close proximity with temptation.

Finn liked to think of himself as a man who possessed a lot of self-control, but one itty-bitty item of clothing in and his willpower already was toast.

"You'd better do it."

"As much as I'd like to argue, I think I'd better, too."

She made fast work of it. The addition of her skirt and top was anticlimactic. He donned his pants. Shirtless and shoeless, he walked her to the door, where she slipped into her heels. From outside came the distant, if distinctive honk of a car horn.

"I think that's for me."

"Let me grab my shirt and I'll walk you down."

While they waited for the elevator to arrive, they eyed one another in silence as the first bit of awkwardness settled in.

Finn had gone on several dates since his divorce, including a few that had ended up back at his place, where the activities that followed were clothing optional. None of those had left him tongue-tied. Of course, none of the sex had been quite as spectacular, the act quite as meaningful or the women quite as important.

The elevator arrived and he pulled the doors apart for her. They were nearly to the ground level when he blurted out, "When will I see you again? I mean, I really think I should make you dinner since I never got around to it."

She turned and smiled. "When do you want to see me again? It doesn't have to be for dinner, although I will hold you to that since you lured me to your apartment under false pretenses." She leaned in then and kissed Finn's cheek. "Thank you, by the way."

"For?"

"Luring me here under false pretenses."

"That was entirely my pleasure." And he took a moment

to thank the heavens she wasn't the sort of female to play hard to get. "How about tomorrow...today, I guess, since it's nearly three in the morning."

"Okay. Want to meet at Isadora's?" she asked. "I'll even let you sleep in. We can meet at nine o'clock. Ten even. I'm flexible."

"Very flexible, as I recall." He grinned and so did she. It was with a great deal of regret that he said, "Unfortunately, my sisters are coming over. That was the text I received earlier. Kristy claims they want to talk about Mom's birthday party, but I figure I'm in for the third degree."

"Ah. That was fast." They arrived at street level and Finn hoisted the door for her. "Joanna was busy while she was tending bar."

"Yeah. Technology has made busybodies' lives a lot simpler," he replied as they started down the hall to the exit. "Before texts and tweets and instant messaging, it would have taken at least a couple of days before they were all brought up to speed on my social life."

"I'm free in the afternoon. Evening, too," she told him. "What about you?"

"Same."

Like Lara, Finn had cleared his schedule for the competition, so he had a lot of free time this week, unless he chose to take on any jobs at the last minute. And he had no intention of taking a job now if it meant he wouldn't be able to spend time with Lara.

That was a sobering thought. It must have showed on his face, because she asked, "Is something wrong?"

"No..." He let the reality settle in and smiled. "Not a thing."

"So, when do we get to meet her?" Kate demanded before she had even cleared the threshold to Finn's apartment.

She was twenty-four and, as the baby of the family, used to getting her way.

Kristy, who was hot on her heels, said, "You're bringing her to Mom's party, right?"

"I—I'm not sure," he told them, surprised to find the answer so ambiguous when "No" was his standard reply when it came to having dates meet his family.

But then, Lara was different, special in a way he had only just begun to fathom. And their "sextracurricular" activities of the night before had his brain as foggy as his body was relaxed.

"Really? So, maybe?" Kate asked. She was already grinning like a Cheshire cat.

He decided to ignore her. "Speaking of Mom's party, what do you think of my gift?"

He'd shot them an email about it the day before in response to their pestering.

"Tap shoes and lessons?" Kristy settled her hands on her hips. "Do you really expect us to believe that you came up with that all on your own?"

"I...could have," he protested.

Kristy blew out a breath and glanced skyward. "Right. And I could come up with the theory of relativity if Einstein hadn't beaten me to it. Come on, Finn. You would have sent a bouquet of flowers or some lame gift certificate for a department store. This has thoughtful stamped all over it. And that means you had help from a woman."

"Forget about how he came up with the idea." Kate waved a hand, as if clearing away smoke. Before he could be grateful for her interference, however, she added, "The point is, he's dating again."

"I've had a few dates since my divorce."

"With easy women you wanted to sleep with but not necessarily ever see again," Kristy put in. She held her hands out, palms up, and added, "I'm not making a judgment. I'm just stating a fact."

"I'm offended."

"You're a guy," she replied blithely.

"Kristy's right," Kate said.

He should have known he couldn't count on her to take his side. His sisters might fight like cats between themselves, but they were a united front when it came to their only brother.

Levering onto one of the tall stools at the island, Kate continued. "I think we should meet her before Mom's party."

"Me, too."

"I don't know," he said slowly.

But Kristy was shaking her head. "You don't get a vote in this."

"If we don't meet her before the party, we'll have to grill her at the party, which will make it no fun for her at all."

"I haven't said for sure that I'm going to bring her."

Kate studied him with eyes so much like their mother's it took an effort not to squirm. Finally, her mouth curved with a grin. "You want to."

Finn gave up. How could he not. She was right. He did want Lara to meet his family and vice versa. Instead of making him nervous, however, admitting it left him feeling settled.

CHAPTER TWELVE

Baste

"YOU'RE GOING ON another date with Finn tonight?" Dana asked. She was seated on the couch in Lara's apartment, eating a bowl of the tomato bisque with homemade croutons that Lara had whipped up for lunch. "How many does that make this week? Is it more than the five you and Finn went on last week."

Not enough, in Lara's estimation. The more time she spent with Finn, the harder it was to be apart. Hours stretched until they felt like days. It was crazy, insane. It was…right.

"You just sighed," Dana accused, pointing the business end of a spoon at Lara.

The best offense was always a good defense, so Lara settled her hands on her hips. "Do you have a problem with that?"

"Yes, I do." Dana pouted. "You've had more dates in the past two weeks than I've had in six months. It's not fair." She grinned then. "But I'm happy for you."

"Thanks, Dana. I'm pretty happy for me, too."

The network still had not decided what to do with Lara's spot on *Executive Chef Challenge*. With the competition still on hiatus, Finn had lots of free time, and he seemed more than happy to spend it with Lara.

They had gone out to dinner a couple more times, and he'd cooked for her in his apartment as promised, making a Bolognese that had been almost as delicious as the love-making that had followed.

She'd never felt like this before. The only dark cloud was the seemingly irreparable rift with her father. Even in that, Finn tried to lift her spirits. Given his close family ties, it was no wonder he was so optimistic that Lara and her father would one day not only be on speaking terms again but would also enjoy a healthy father-daughter relationship.

Lara fussed with the slim silver belt at the waist of her red A-line dress. The outfit was new right down to the strappy three-inch heels on her feet. It wasn't like her to worry about her appearance so much. Usually she just went with whatever her hand touched first when she reached into the closet. Her strategy worked because the bulk of her wardrobe was limited to mix-and-match separates in largely neutral shades.

But tonight…tonight seemed to call for even more care than dressing for an evening at the theater had the previous week, which was why she'd gone shopping earlier in the day.

She fussed with the silver belt again. It hadn't come with the dress. She'd bought it on the saleswoman's recommendation. Same for the sparkly chandelier earrings that caught the light whenever she turned.

"Do you think this is too much?"

"I think you look fabulous, and if I were four sizes smaller and six inches shorter, I would be asking to borrow that dress. Same for the shoes. The peep-toe thing is very sexy. Are they new?"

"Relatively," she averred.

"Well, they get a thumbs-up." She held up the digit in question. "I'd give them two, but that would require me to put down the bowl. This… What did you call it?"

"Bisque."

"Right. Bisque." She nodded. "It's divine."

"Thanks. It's not hard to make. I can show you how."

"That's okay." Dana shook her head. "We've gone that route before. Nothing I make ever turns out the way it does for you, even when I faithfully follow the recipe. Besides, I'd rather come over and raid your fridge. There's always something amazing in there to reheat. And the bonus, I don't have to do dishes."

"Maybe I should start collecting a cover charge at the door."

"I'd pay it without a second thought. In the meantime, I'll just offer free advice." She enjoyed a spoonful of bisque before continuing. "You asked if the dress is too much. I can't answer that without knowing what you're doing and where you will be doing it."

Dana bobbed her eyebrows, making it impossible to keep a straight face. Even as she sent her gaze skyward, Lara was smiling.

"Finn is taking me to a birthday party."

"That's the what. I need the where. Restaurant? Banquet hall? And who is the party for? A child? His best friend?"

Lara nibbled the inside of her cheek as she debated the wisdom of being completely forthright with her friend, who was known to jump to conclusions. Nerves got the upper hand on her better judgment.

"It's for his mom. She's turning sixty and his family is getting together at his boyhood home in Queens to celebrate."

"Oh." Her friend's eyes widened and her mouth stayed in a circle after uttering that single syllable. "You've known one another for less than three weeks and he's taking you to meet his parents."

"No, no, no." Lara was quick with the denial. "Finn

is not taking me to meet his parents. He's taking me to a birthday party."

"For his mother." Dana nodded. "And mothers are also known as parents."

"Okay, but it's her party, so, sure, she's going to be there." Lara swallowed.

As would Finn's father...

And his two sisters...

And an assortment of aunts, uncles, cousins and close family friends...

Finn might have mentioned something about a grand-parent or two as well, but, of course, by that point, Lara had been concentrating so hard on not hyperventilating that she couldn't recall the particulars. For that matter, her breathing was becoming a little erratic now.

It didn't help matters when Dana said again, "Lara, please. He's taking you to meet his parents!"

This time, she spoke slowly and several decibels louder, as if Lara were not only dim but practically deaf, as well.

"It's not like that. I mean, I think we're getting kind of serious, sure, but we haven't known one another very long."

"You barely knew Jeffrey when you agreed to marry him."

Lara shook her head, feeling somewhat relieved by the comparison.

"That's exactly my point. Jeffrey was a huge mistake, one that I made willfully and with the express purpose of irritating my father. You can't rush real relationships. And the fact that both of us have been married before—"

"Finn was married, too? You didn't mention that."

And Lara wasn't about to get into the details now, but then her friend asked, "How long has it been over?"

Lara replied, "Long enough. He's not among the walk-ing wounded."

"Just be sure," Dana said, her face etched with concern,

and no wonder. Dana's last serious boyfriend had dumped her after admitting he was still in love with his former fiancée.

"I am sure when it comes to that. Positive, in fact. But I don't know where this is heading."

"Where do you want it to head?"

Because the answer that sprang immediately to mind left her feeling dazed, Lara replied, "I'm enjoying myself. I'm happy. That's enough for now."

"For now."

Rather than making Lara feel better, Dana's agreement left her yearning for permanence.

"Did you hear me?" Her friend snapped a finger in front of Lara's face. "I asked if I get to meet him."

"If I say no, will it matter?"

Dana just grinned.

Finn's breath caught when Lara opened her apartment door. He'd once thought of her looks as understated. Well, nothing about them could be classified as such now. She'd played up her eyes with some sort of makeup magic, and even though she'd left her hair down, it was pulled back on the sides to showcase a pair of dangling earrings. The dress, in va-va-va-voom red, wasn't curve-hugging, but that hardly mattered. It cinched in at the waist before flowing away from her hips and ending just above the knee.

His immediate thought was *What does she have on underneath it?*

It was a question he fully intended to answer for himself later.

"Wow!" His exclamation came out in an exhaled rush.

"Too much?" she asked, frowning.

"Too perfect."

She smiled, looking every bit as pleased now as she had appeared uncertain a moment earlier. "Thank you."

He was leaning in to kiss her when he spied the tall brunette. She had a spoon in her mouth and what he construed as approval brimming in her eyes. He stopped, straightened and worked up a smile. "Hi."

The brunette put the spoon in the bowl she was holding and grinned. "Hello."

"Finn, this is my friend Dana," Lara said. "She lives in an apartment down the hall."

"It's nice to meet you," he said, giving the woman's hand a brief press.

"The same. So, Lara tells me you're taking her to meet your—"

"A birthday party," Lara cut in. "We're going to a birthday party."

"For his mother."

"She's turning sixty," Lara added with an overly bright smile. "Don't you have to be going now?"

"Right. Laundry awaits. Wouldn't want to be late for *that*."

She was two steps out the door when she popped back in and handed Lara the spoon and empty bowl. "Thanks for another delicious meal." To Finn, she said, "Lara feeds me. In fact, with as much as she cooks, I think she feeds half of the tenants in this building."

This time as she exited, Finn saw her flash a discreet thumbs-up in Lara's direction.

"Sorry about that," Lara said once they were alone in her apartment.

"That's all right. I take it I passed muster?"

"I was hoping you hadn't seen that." She groaned and apologized a second time.

He decided to change the subject. Motioning with his chin, he asked, "So, what was in the bowl?"

"Tomato bisque with homemade croutons. It was my father's recipe, but I've made a couple of changes to it over the years." She rattled off an unexpected combination of spices that sounded amazing. "If you're pressed for an appetizer idea on the show, it makes an excellent first course."

"I'll have to get the recipe from you," Finn replied, although at the moment he had something more delectable in mind when it came to first courses.

He took the bowl and set it aside. Then he pulled her against him. The move was akin to striking a match. Something caught, flared even before their mouths met.

Finn intended the kiss to be hot. He saw no point in pretending he didn't want their date to end with Lara beneath him on a mattress, moaning with pleasure. So, yes, he intended it to be hot, but brief, too, since they had a party to get to, one that they'd just barely make on time even with traffic on their side. But as soon as he felt Lara's arms encircle his neck, he knew brief wasn't in the cards. He had a better chance of extinguishing a bonfire with kerosene than quashing this hormone-fueled inferno.

He had the skirt of the dress he'd admired already rucked up to her waist before the kiss ended. The tips of his fingers were flirting with her panties when he felt her hands tug at his belt.

"Great minds," he murmured.

"Do we have time?"

"I think so."

A throaty chuckle ensued, and she asked, "And which head might you be thinking with, Finn?"

"The only one that counts right now." He marched her backward several paces and glanced around. The couch was handy, but not very big. He wanted space. Room to spread out.

"Bedroom?" she asked.

Great minds, definitely. He nodded.

"Second door on the right," she told him and then let

out a squeal of surprise when Finn scooped her up in his arms and carried her there.

"I've never been swept off my feet before," Lara remarked as he started down the short hallway.

"The gesture seems appropriate, not to mention expedient."

"I thought maybe it was intended to be romantic."

"That, too," he replied on a grin as he entered her bedroom.

It was a typical size for Manhattan, which meant it barely accommodated her bed with just enough left on either side for floating nightstands. This was especially the case since the bed in question was king-size. He'd hoped for room. Wish granted.

"You have a very big bed," he murmured in appreciation, as he deposited her on the side that was not covered in clothes.

"You'll have to excuse the mess. I wasn't sure what to wear and I changed several times before realizing…" Lara's voice trailed away.

"That this outfit was the one," he finished, giving the hemline a nudge north.

She made a strangled sound when his fingers trailed over the sensitive skin on the insides of her thighs.

"N-n-no. More like that I needed to go shopping."

"It's a nice dress."

Finn decided he would let her remove it, lest he rip it to pieces in his haste. In the meantime, he peeled off his sports coat.

"The shoes are new, too," she said, drawing his gaze to sexy heels. She toed them off slowly, letting first one and then the other drop to the floor. The muffled thud they made on the rug was no match for the loud pounding of his heart.

"I like those, too," he managed.

Even if they weren't quite stiletto height, the heels she'd been wearing were a definite turn-on, especially on a woman who he was pretty sure didn't don them often.

But Lara had done so for him.

And she'd gone to the trouble of shopping for a new dress, too. For their date. He found her candor every bit as appealing as the tantalizing view of her thighs that her prone pose on the mattress revealed.

He had plans for those thighs. Big plans. And so he got busy with the buttons of his shirt.

He hadn't bothered with a tie. He wasn't the sort of man who felt comfortable wearing one, although he owned several, and when the occasion demanded it, he not only put one on but could also manage a passable Windsor knot. This occasion did not. His mother wouldn't expect such formality from her son or any of the other men at her birthday celebration. And Finn was exceedingly glad for that now since it meant one less article of clothing for him to remove.

His shirt was shed in short order, and then he started on his pants. Lara was on her knees on the bed now, tugging the dress over her head. She emerged from beneath the fabric with her hair mussed, her expression eager and the miserly scraps of red satin that passed for undergarments making his mouth go slack even as other parts of his body turned rigid.

"I was wondering what you had on under that dress."

"Like?"

He swallowed. "Oh, yeah."

She smiled in response, and when he just stood there ogling her like some oversexed teenager, she prodded, "Do you need help with your pants?"

He blinked, cleared his throat. Before he could respond, though, she had taken matters into her own hands—literally—by reaching for the end of the belt that she had so eagerly unbuckled during their kiss in the living room. Lara gave it a yank, pulling it free with a flourish.

Finn unzipped his fly. "I think I can take it from here," he told her.

They were late for the party.

Lara had known they would be the moment Finn swept her up into his arms and carried her to the bedroom. She hadn't cared then. She'd been too desperate and turned on to have second thoughts. She had them now as they walked through the front door of his boyhood home.

They hadn't cleared the foyer when they were descended upon by a pair of young women. The sisters he'd warned her about, Lara decided, based on their similar coloring and facial features.

"They can smell fear," he leaned close and whispered into her ear.

She was pretty sure he was kidding.

Lara worked up a smile as the first wave of the inquisition began.

"Finn, you're late." The taller of the two women announced before sticking out her hand, "I'm Kate. Finn's favorite sister. It's nice to *finally* meet you."

Kate sent Finn a meaningful look.

"Thank you. The sa—"

"Kristy."

This woman was shorter, appeared younger. But when she grabbed Lara's hand, her grip was firm almost to the point of painful. For a moment, Lara wondered if Kristy intended to arm wrestle. But then she let go.

"We've been dying to meet you," Kate said.

"Yeah." Kristy nodded. "We wanted to have lunch earlier in the week, but Finn said you were busy."

"Oh?" She cast an amused glance in his direction.

Joanna came up then. "Lara!"

She didn't bother with a handshake. She wrapped Lara in a bone-crushing hug, literally picking her up off the ground.

"All right. All right. Put her down," Finn said. When Lara's feet hit the floor, he told them, "Back off and give her some breathing space."

She might have appreciated his interference, but now that his sisters and cousin no longer had her boxed in, she had the full attention of the large crowd that filled the living room.

"Will you look at that! Griffin brought a date," an older woman said. Her warbly voice boomed in the suddenly quiet room.

"Sorry," Finn murmured. "My grandmother won't admit it, but she's a little hard of hearing."

Kate leaned in close to add, "Yeah. I'm pretty sure she thought she was whispering."

"Are all of these people related to you?" Lara asked Finn.

Even if she were to add in all of the relatives on the farthest branches of her family tree, she doubted she could come up with this many people. Her mother was an only child. And her father had only one sister, whose husband had died before Lara was born. They'd had no children. The Westbrook gene pool, meanwhile, seemed as vast as the Atlantic. Not only was the living room packed, but more people were spilling in from the doorways to other parts of the house. It was amazing.... It was terrifying.

"Uh, Finn. She looks like she could use a drink," Kristy noted, her tone wry.

"I'll get her one. Which would you prefer?" Joanna asked. "A beer or a glass of wine?"

"Yes." Lara nodded, too dazed to make an actual choice.

Dimly, she was aware of Finn telling his cousin to bring a glass of merlot.

"Where's Mom?" he then asked Kate, whose face split into a grin.

"Where do you think?"

"Come on." He grabbed Lara's hand. "We're heading to the kitchen."

Lara took a deep breath as they left the relative safety of the foyer and waded into the throng of guests. She might not know where the kitchen was located, but even without Finn to guide her, she figured she could have found it simply by following her nose. A tantalizing mix of herbs spiced the air. Garlic, rosemary and thyme were the obvious ones. Lara inhaled deeply, this time to savor the aroma rather than to quell her nerves.

"Something smells marvelous."

He winked. "If you think it smells good, just wait till you taste it."

They didn't get far before someone clapped Finn on the back in greeting. Then another person pulled him in for a bear hug. Kisses were exchanged as readily as her parents used to trade thinly veiled insults.

All the while, Finn took the time to introduce Lara to each and every one of them. Never would she remember all of their names. In fact, other than his sisters and Joanna, she'd already forgotten them. There simply were too many and she was overwhelmed. The feeling had less to do with the sheer number of kin and close friends that had gathered under one roof to wish his mother a happy birthday, and more to do with camaraderie and caring on display. She'd never experienced anything remotely like this. Indeed, she'd assumed it existed only in books and movies. But it was real, tangible and beautiful in a way that made her ache.

When they reached his grandmother, the older woman pinched Finn's cheeks with her arthritic fingers.

"And who might this pretty young woman be?" she asked before he could get out a word.

"This is Lara Dunham, Grandma." He leaned down toward her ear and said it loudly. In a wry voice he added, "I'm surprised my sisters haven't mentioned her."

She waved a hand in a dismissive fashion. "They talk too fast and are always muttering half under their breath. How is an old woman supposed to hear anything they say?"

"It's nice to meet you, Mrs. Westbrook," Lara said.

The older woman gave her the once-over with a pair of rheumy eyes. "That remains to be seen, my dear girl. That remains to be seen."

Lara was taken aback, but caught herself before she could laugh. And thank God, because the older woman was dead serious. She was glad for the glass of wine Finn's cousin handed her just then.

Lara fortified herself with a sip as Finn whisked her to the kitchen, throwing out introductions in haphazard fashion as he propelled her through a pack of chattering aunts and female cousins to a woman who stood in front of the stove, patiently stirring a pot of something. The man beside her was an older version of Finn—same handsome face, if more weathered and refined.

"Finish up already, Mary," he said. "Your guests don't care if the gravy has a few lumps. They're here to see you."

"You can't rush good gravy," she protested with a shake of her head. Then she turned and her gaze fell on Finn. "Griffin, you made it!"

"Of course I made it. I wouldn't miss your party, Mom. Happy birthday."

"I expected you an hour ago." She cocked an eyebrow after saying so. "You said you'd help with any last-minute dinner preparations."

"I… Um." He glanced at Lara, who felt her face catch fire. "Traffic," he lied. "We ran into a big backup on the way over."

The older man grinned. Neither of his parents appeared convinced, but the matter was promptly dropped.

"Well, I'm glad you're here now. And that you brought your...*friend*."

Mary said it the same way Joanna had when they'd met in Spanky's.

"This is Lara. Lara, my parents, Mary and Donovan Westbrook."

His mother handed the whisk to Finn so she could shake Lara's hand. She didn't let go afterward. Instead, she steered Lara out the back door onto the duplex's deck, leaving her son to tend to the gravy. Her husband followed them.

"My daughters tell me you're a chef," she began.

"I am. Yes."

"Finn is very gifted."

Lara nodded.

"You know he was married before, right?"

"Mary."

But she shushed her husband and held Lara's gaze.

"Yes. He told me."

"She was a chef, too."

"Mary."

This time she waved a hand at Donovan before continuing. "She broke his heart, stole his recipes, even the ones that came from our family, and damaged his reputation."

Lara cleared her throat. "He told me that, too."

"Good. His heart has mended. He's creative enough to come up with new recipes. And his reputation... Well, he's doing his damnedest to see that restored. As his mother, it pained me to see him put through hell. I am relieved to see his life turning around. So you will understand when I warn you that if you hurt him, I will hurt you."

She smiled so beautifully afterward that Lara might have thought she'd heard wrong, but Finn's father had closed his eyes and was groaning.

Finn came outside and rescued her then.

"Hey, Mom. Gravy's ready, and the roast looks rested enough for Dad to start slicing."

Once they were alone, he said, "So, what did my mom say to you?"

"Oh, nothing much." Lara lifted her shoulders in a negligible shrug that belied her words when she added, "She just threatened me with bodily injury if I did anything to hurt you."

The corners of his eyes crinkled with his laughter. "She did not."

"Uh-huh." To her mortification, her eyes grew moist.

"Lara? Hey, it's okay. She didn't really mean it."

"Yes, she did." But that wasn't why Lara had started to cry. She rose on her tiptoes to give Finn a quick kiss. "You are so lucky."

CHAPTER THIRTEEN

Let stand

"YOU'RE QUIET," FINN said as they drove back to the city later that night.

"Just tired," Lara murmured. Her head was back against the rest. Despite the car's dim interior, she looked exhausted. She turned toward him and smiled. "I haven't talked that much in one evening since…ever."

"Westbrook women are an insanely chatty bunch," he agreed.

But Finn knew it was more than that. Lara was overwhelmed. He was pretty sure he knew the reason.

"Your mother really liked your gift," she said.

That was an understatement. Upon opening the card, Mary had laughed and then dabbed her eyes before starting to cry in earnest. Just when Finn had begun having second thoughts about giving her tap lessons, she'd stood up and executed a brief toe-heel, toe-heel slide combination on the living room's scuffed oak planking. She hadn't liked the gift. She'd loved it.

He let go of the steering wheel with his right hand so he could run his knuckles lightly over Lara's cheek. "Thanks again for your insights."

"Glad I could help."

Finn wanted to help her, too. A germ of an idea began to

form, a plan to be executed at a later date. It needed more time to gel. He tucked it away.

"Are you coming up?" she asked as they drew closer to her apartment building. "I have a bottle of that red wine you sold me on just waiting to be opened."

His answer was to pull into the first available parking spot along the curb.

It was well after midnight when Finn crumpled into a heap beside her on the mattress. He felt totally sapped of his strength but, in an odd way, energized, too.

He tilted his head to the side and studied her profile in the low light. For the past couple of years, his goal had been to rebuild his reputation so that he could once again run his own restaurant. He'd come up with new recipes and a new name for the place. He'd mulled over potential marketing strategies. He'd even fiddled with ideas for front-of-the-house decor, color schemes and flow. He'd been single-minded, driven.

Now, in a remarkably short period of time, his focus had expanded to include something, or rather, someone else.

"You're staring," she said. Her mouth curved, though, telling him that his breach in manners hadn't offended her.

"I can't help it. You're beautiful."

It was more than her looks, though. Finn knew that. In fact, he'd reached that conclusion long before they'd left the network studio on the first day.

Destiny's timing might suck, but it couldn't be denied. God help him, he was falling in love.

She rolled to her side, levered up on one elbow. In the room's dim light, her fair skin glowed almost translucently.

"It's been a long time since I felt beautiful," she admitted quietly. "It's been a long time since I felt…anything, Finn."

"I know exactly what you mean. The same here."

Her smile turned circumspect. "If I'm beautiful now, it's because you make me happy. So, thank you for that."

It wasn't gratitude he was after, but he understood what she meant. He was happy, too. Hell, he hadn't realized how lonely and miserable he'd been until she'd come into his life.

He cupped his hand to the side of her head and rubbed his thumb across her cheek before pulling her to him for a kiss. When it ended, she was sprawled over his chest and his body had already begun to ache with need.

"Does this mean you're ready for round two?" she asked on a throaty chuckle that he felt as much as heard.

Turned on? He was past that point. As quickly as he could, Finn rolled and changed their positions so that she was now pinned beneath him.

"You know," he told her, as his rigid body melded to her softness, "technically, this is round three."

He stayed the night. She hadn't asked him to…exactly. Although the one time he'd gotten up to go to the bathroom, she'd sighed heavily in her sleep. When he'd returned to the bed afterward, she'd snuggled against his side, her body warm and welcoming and far too inviting to even consider leaving.

When he woke in the morning, he was alone in the bed. He pulled on the boxers he found on the floor and followed the familiar sound of a sharp knife meeting a cutting board's surface. Lara was in the kitchen, standing with her back to him at the room's small prep space. She was wearing his shirt…and nothing else, as far as his imagination was concerned.

His gaze took in the shapely line of her legs, including the delicate curve of her ankle. He'd never considered himself an ankle man, but she had a nice pair. In fact, everything about her ticked the boxes on his fantasy wish list.

"Hungry?" she asked without turning around.

Finn merely laughed at that.

"I meant for food." She did face him now, holding a wickedly sharp knife in one hand. Some men might have found that off-putting. Not Finn, of course.

"What are you making?"

"I'm not sure, yet. I was thinking about Greek omelets. But I can go with something else if you're not a fan of feta cheese."

"I love feta," he said, drawing closer to give her a proper good-morning kiss.

On the cutting board, he noticed that she'd already sliced up a green pepper and some fresh oregano.

"I'm happy to help," he offered.

For an answer, she pulled a knife from the magnetic strip on the backsplash and handed it to him. By mutual agreement, they decided to leave out the red onion. While she whisked half a dozen eggs and a dash of milk into the perfect consistency, he diced a ripe tomato and sliced up kalamata olives.

They worked well together, talking as they went.

"What do you like the most about cooking?" she asked, as she poured the egg mixture into an omelet pan.

"Working with knives." Finn grinned maniacally and held up the lethal-looking blade he'd been using.

"Besides the sharp implements."

He gave that some serious thought. "I guess I like the science behind it."

"Science?" Lara glanced over at his answer.

"Yeah. If you do A and B, then you wind up with C."

She tilted her head to one side. "There are some variables thrown in."

"True, but not that many. And most of them can be controlled. If you buy a quality cut of meat, add the perfect mix and amount of spices, then grill it at the right temperature for the right amount of time, you're going to end up with a really good steak."

She nodded. "I guess I appreciate the control aspect, too."

"But that's not why you love to cook," he guessed.

"I like cooking for the same reason I like styling food. It's creative."

"Art on a plate."

"Exactly." She grinned.

"Okay, Picasso." He pointed his knife at the ingredients on the countertop. "Show me what you got."

They ate breakfast in her tiny living room, trading war stories from culinary school. It turned out they'd had a couple of the same instructors, albeit a few years apart. Afterward, Finn helped Lara set her kitchen to rights. It was closing in on noon when he decided to spring on her the idea that had begun to germinate the previous night.

She offered the perfect segue when she asked, "Are you getting excited about tomorrow?"

Finally, the competition was set to get under way.

Finn didn't know how the network planned to deal with Lara's absence. Were they simply going to move ahead with eleven chefs? Or had they reinstated a previously eliminated contestant? Regardless, the competition was to start back up bright and early Monday.

"Sure. I'm excited."

"Nervous?"

He shook his head. "Excited," he said again.

She winked. "You just keep telling yourself that."

"You know, I was thinking…" He folded the dishcloth he was holding in half and looped it over the handle to the oven.

"About?"

He cleared his throat, met her eye. "About doing a little recon today."

"Recon?"

"Yeah. Reconnaissance. You know, get the lay of the land at my future place of employment." He offered up what he hoped was a charmingly cocky grin.

"Are you talking about going to the Chesterfield?"

"You catch on fast," he teased.

"Why?"

"It's been a while since I was last in there."

"Is that the only reason?"

"No," he admitted. "So, what do you say? Want to tag along?"

She took her time drying the chopping board. Just when he was sure that her answer would be no, she glanced up and smiled. "I should warn you. My father threatened to have me forcibly removed from the premises the last time I was in his restaurant. Are you sure you want me to come?" Her laugher was strained when she added, "For that matter, are you sure you want to be seen with me? He might hold it against you. And believe me, if anyone knows how to hold a grudge, it's my father."

Her points were valid, but nothing that Finn hadn't already considered.

"I'll take my chances," he told her. "So, will you come?"

"As long as you're sure."

"I'm positive."

Before Finn went home to shower and change, he and Lara made plans to meet outside the Chesterfield at three o'clock. That would put them in the dining room after the Sunday brunch and lunch crowd, but well before the dinner rush.

Lara paced the sidewalk in front of the Chesterfield as she waited for Finn to arrive. He wasn't late. She was early.

And she was nervous, as evidenced by her agitated pacing and moist palms.

It was silly, really, not to mention pointless to be this keyed up. It wasn't as if she had anything left to lose. Her father had made his feelings plain where his only child was concerned. Lara was dead to him. It didn't get much more finite than that. Yet she couldn't help but hope, foolish as it might be, that someday he would change his mind. She kept thinking about Finn with his big, boisterous family, and all of the love and affection that had been unabashedly on display. If she could have but a morsel of that…it would be enough.

Before they'd left his parents' home at the end of the evening, his mother and sisters had given Finn hugs and kisses. No surprise there, since that was how they had greeted him, too. Heck, it was how practically everyone at the party had greeted him at one point or another. And they'd hugged Lara, too.

But the real surprise came when his dad wrapped his son in an embrace as they were leaving. Afterward, he'd kissed Finn's cheek and said, "I love you."

Three words said without a hint of embarrassment, without the least bit of reservation, without any qualification. And Finn had said them right back.

Lara couldn't imagine her father being so open with either his feelings or his affection. Even when she was a child, he'd been stingy with both. Today, she was hoping he also would withhold his displeasure.

"Lara!" Finn called her name as he stepped from the cab.

She smiled and relaxed a little, until she saw what he was wearing.

She'd gone with black dress pants and a block-print silk top. The wedge heels weren't high, but they added a couple of inches to her height and kept the hem of her pant legs from dragging on the ground.

Finn was dressed in khakis and a long-sleeved button-down shirt, whose cuffs had been rolled to the middle of his forearms. He looked gorgeous, but the Chesterfield required formal attire. No jacket, no tie…no service. And no exceptions. Her father had once refused admittance to a Grammy-winning artist who'd shown up in his signature black cowboy hat and embellished Western shirt.

"Forget something?" she asked.

He frowned a moment before the realization dawned. Then he uttered a mild oath.

"We can do this another time," Lara said, feeling the noose around her neck go slack.

But Finn shook his head. "I need a new sports coat and tie anyway. Come on."

He grabbed her hand. They cut across Forty-Fourth Street to Fifth Avenue and then headed several blocks to Saks.

"I can't believe we're going clothes shopping now."

He held open the door. "Uh, let me set the record straight. Women go shopping for clothes. Men go and buy them. Totally different process."

"How do you figure that?"

"I'll show you."

He led the way to the men's department. Within five minutes of reaching his destination, he had picked out a tie and, after finding his size, was pulling on a jacket. Once it was on, he put out his arms to test the give across the back, and then dropped them to his sides so he could take note of where the cuffs hit just below his wrists.

"This works without having to be altered. Let's go."

Lara blinked. "You don't want to look around some more, maybe try on a couple other things just to be sure?"

"No. See, that's the difference between men and women. Women go to a store to shop and men go to buy."

He smiled after offering his explanation. Lara wanted to disagree with him, but she couldn't. He had a point.

Twenty minutes later, they were back at the Chesterfield, being shown to their table by a woman Lara didn't recognize. She was glad for that, since it meant the woman likely didn't recognize her either. Soon enough, her father would find out she was here, trespassing. She just hoped that the scene to follow—and she did not doubt there would be a scene—would be less humiliating than the one in the network's kitchen.

They were seated at a two-top that might have been intimate were it not in the middle of the dining room. Of course, at this time of day, only a smattering of tables was filled anyway. The hostess handed them a pair of leatherbound menus before heading off.

Lara opened her menu, holding it up high enough to obscure her from the view of the kitchen. She had little doubt her father was in there, preparing for the dinner rush.

"The specials sound good, especially the grilled sea bass," Finn remarked.

She read over the description. "My father is a big fan of grilling, especially when it comes to fish. Something to keep in mind in the competition."

"Duly noted," Finn said. Then his gaze was drawn to a point behind Lara.

"My father?" she asked before Finn could say anything.

He nodded. "And he doesn't look happy."

The surprise would be if he had. Lara set down her menu and, though she knew it would look as forced as it felt, she smiled. Turning in her seat, she met her fate head-on.

"Hi, Dad."

"What are you doing here?" Clifton's voice was unnaturally low, and a vein throbbed at his temple.

"Having an early dinner. I was thinking the sea bass. It

sounds excellent. I was just telling Finn that grilling is one of the Chesterfield's specialties."

"You're not welcome here," he told her between gritted teeth.

"I know that."

"Then why are you here?" he demanded again. This time his voice rose enough that the patrons seated at a table nearby glanced their way.

"It's my doing, sir." Finn rose to his feet. "I asked Lara to come with me."

"You...look familiar."

"Finn Westbrook." He held out a hand, which her father pointedly ignored. "I'm one of the chefs competing for the chance to run your kitchen."

That received a snort. "You have a hell of a lot of nerve showing up here with *her*."

Finn lowered his hand, but he didn't back down. In fact, he took a slight step forward. Her father outweighed him by a good fifty pounds, but Finn was at least a couple of inches taller.

"Why?" he asked baldly, although the friendly smile that accompanied his words kept them from being too menacing. "I admire your restaurant and I respect you enough as a chef to want to run the Chesterfield's kitchen. So, naturally, I want to eat here and see how my cooking style will meld."

"She is not welcome here, and neither are you if you're with her."

"*She* is your daughter."

"I don't have a daughter." After that pronouncement, he rubbed his chest.

Lara was on her feet in an instant, her own heart thumping as she worried over his. "Dad, are you okay?"

He shrugged off the hand she'd placed on his arm. "I'm fine. Or I will be once you're gone."

If he'd inserted a knife between her shoulder blades and

given it a few ruthless twists, it would have been less painful. Still, her reception here was no less than she'd expected.

"I'm going." She hesitated only a moment before telling him, "I know I've said I'm sorry, but there's something else I want you to know. I love you, Dad."

Finn watched Lara walk away. Her head was up, her shoulders squared. He wasn't fooled in the least. She was gutted. And he was just plain pissed.

He turned to Clifton. "She does, you know. What does she have to do to prove herself worthy of your love?"

"Stay out of it," the older man warned gruffly, but he looked as if he'd been sucker punched.

Finn ignored Clifton's order and went on. "She's made mistakes. Some pretty big ones, from what she's told me. But I don't think she's the only one who put strain on your relationship."

"You know nothing of our relationship!"

"I know your daughter wishes that you had one," he shot back. "I know she's been reaching out to you, trying to patch things up. I also know that the two of you have a lot in common."

That earned a scoffing noise.

"Lara loves cooking as much as you do, Mr. Chesterfield. And she's damned good at it."

"She styles food." Clifton's tone was condescending.

Finn's hands balled into fists at his sides, but he went on. "Your daughter's skill and passion for cooking, both of those come from you. If you gave her half a chance, you'd see that."

Clifton tilted his head to one side and regarded Finn. "You seem to care a great deal about Lara."

"I do."

"Yet you're after the job she wants. How does that sit with you?"

"I…"

"Are you glad she's no longer in the competition?"

Because he wasn't sure how to answer that, Finn replied, "I care a great deal about Lara. I want her to be happy. All I'm saying is I think you should give her a second chance."

CHAPTER FOURTEEN

Cool to room temperature

LARA LEANED AGAINST the mailbox near the street and watched the traffic on Fifth Avenue while she waited for Finn to join her.

When she'd left the restaurant, she'd assumed he was right behind her. But several minutes passed before the door pushed open and he came out. She was grateful for the time to pull herself together. She had her emotions under control. Finn, meanwhile, looked as if he'd taken a surprise punch to the gut.

"Are you okay?" she asked, giving his arm a squeeze.

"That's supposed to be my line," he replied ruefully and pulled her close for a brief hug. "God, Lara, I'm sorry for bringing you here. Obviously, that didn't go as I'd hoped. I guess I thought…"

He shrugged and left the words unsaid.

"You thought you could reason with my father the way you might reason with your own."

"Yeah." He frowned. "I guess I did."

But their families and the dynamics at work within them were totally different. Lara accepted that. Maybe it also was time to accept that she could do nothing to change her fa-

ther's mind about her or to mend their rift. In fact, the more
she tried, the wider it seemed to become.

They grabbed a bite to eat at a deli a few blocks away. They
were overdressed for the casual atmosphere and Lara didn't
have much of an appetite. She picked at her turkey Reuben,
but most of it wound up going into the trash.

Still, Lara used the time to give Finn a few pointers
about her father's preferences and peculiarities when it
came to his restaurant. Even though Clifton wouldn't be
judging the contestants' food, later in the competition he
would be present and have some input.

After today's debacle, she worried that Finn had dug
himself into a hole that even his stellar culinary skills could
not dig him out of.

It was nearly six when she headed home. Finn insisted on
accompanying her to her building. The gesture was sweet,
if unnecessary, especially since he wouldn't be staying.
He had a lot on his mind and an early morning looming.

"Tomorrow's a big day for you," she told him as they
stood outside her apartment door.

"Yeah."

"Call me when you leave the studio?"

"As soon as I clear the lobby," he promised.

"Good luck." She leaned in and kissed him, drawing
back slowly afterward.

As tempting as it was to ask him to stay, she managed
to unlock the door and tell him goodbye.

It was barely eight o'clock, but Finn had been up since
well before dawn and at the studio since just before seven
o'clock. In the greenroom, a large urn of coffee and a tray of
pastries had been set out on a sideboard. Finn had forgone
the sweets and limited himself to two cups of the coffee.

He figured he would need steely nerves and steady hands for the competition.

He worked well under pressure. At least he liked to think he did. But there was no denying that his palms were damp and his heart was kicking out a few extra beats as he waited with the other chefs for the competition to start.

Adding to his nerves was the fact that he'd called Lara twice—once the previous night just before going to bed and again on his way to the studio that morning. Both times her cell phone had rung several times before going to voice mail.

Was she okay?

She'd been pretty distraught after the incident with her father, but she'd rallied afterward and had seemed fine when he'd left her at her apartment. Had something happened?

As Finn stewed over that, he listened with half an ear to the gossip in the greenroom over what the show's new format would be now that they were one contestant short. No one seemed to know, but speculation was rampant that a new development had cropped up since they had been left cooling their heels for another hour.

"Something's going on," he overheard Angel tell Ryder.

The big man grunted. To no one in particular he said, "Let's get this over with already."

Finn was in agreement. He was in his element in a kitchen. Standing here, waiting, he felt frustrated.

The door opened. He expected to see Tristan or one of the interns who'd stopped in twice already to check on the coffee. To his absolute shock, Lara walked into the greenroom. She was dressed casually in cotton pants, flat shoes and a pale blue tunic. She'd pulled her hair back into a no-nonsense ponytail. A slight sheen of gloss drew his gaze briefly to the mouth that knew how to drive him insane.

"What's she doing here?" Ryder's voice rose over the murmurings of the other contestants.

The question was on the tip of Finn's tongue, too. Their gazes met and he noticed the shadows under her eyes.

Had she come down to wish him luck again? That seemed doubtful, given her expression, which was tentative...guilty?

"Lara?" Her name finally made it past his lips. But the growing tension in the room turned it into a question.

Before she could say anything, Tristan strode in and stood next to her. He tucked his clipboard under one arm and clapped his hands together in his signature gesture.

"Chefs, chefs, your attention, please," he called out as if every eye in the place wasn't already trained on him. "Several of you have asked me this morning what the network decided to do about Lara's position in the competition. To fill or not to fill," he added dramatically and then paused for effect. "The network has decided to leave that up to you."

"To us?" someone said.

"What do you mean?" another person asked.

"Does this mean you won't be bringing back a chef from one of the preliminary rounds?" yet another wanted to know.

Finn listened absently to the chatter going on around him as he absorbed the news, still uncertain what to make of Lara's presence.

"Quiet, please. And I'll explain," Tristan was saying. "First of all, no, none of the previously eliminated chefs will be rejoining us. Instead, we've decided it will be up to the eleven of you to decide if Lara stays in the competition."

The room erupted into chaos then.

"You postponed the show for two weeks and *that's* what you've come up with?" Ryder demanded.

"That's not fair!" another chef exclaimed.

"Why bother with a competition at all?" Angel wanted to know.

"Yeah. Why doesn't Daddy just hand over the keys to his kitchen now and be done with it?" Ryder made a scoffing sound before adding, "We all know that's what's going to happen in the end."

Based on what Finn had witnessed at the Chesterfield the previous afternoon, he doubted that would be the case, but something still seemed off. He just couldn't put his finger on what it might be.

"I can assure you, the fix is not in. Lara will compete for the position the same as all of you. For that matter, the same as she had been doing all along. If she wins—"

"When, you mean," Angel snapped.

Tristan's tone held firm. "*If* she wins, it will be because she has proved herself to the judges, and her father *is not* a judge."

"As if he has no pull," someone muttered.

"You said we get to decide," Finn said quietly.

Lara glanced at him briefly. From her expression, he couldn't figure out what she was thinking. But again he got the impression she felt guilty.

"That's right," Tristan said. "The network decided to let the eleven of you vote on the matter."

Finn glanced around the room. He had a pretty good idea where Angel, Ryder and a couple of other chefs stood based on the comments that had been made. That put the tally at four who wanted her gone for sure. As for the rest, it was a tougher call.

"The network is aware of your concerns about fairness. That's why, if you decide to allow Lara to compete, the rules will be tweaked to accommodate her presence and quell any doubts about favoritism."

"Tweaked how?" Angel asked.

"The judging will be blind. The panel will not know which chef prepared which dish."

"Right," Ryder muttered. "Enough talk. Let's vote."

"Before you do that, Lara wanted to say a few words."

Tristan stepped aside, granting her the floor. Her nerves were palpable as she cleared her throat and wrung her hands.

"First of all, I want to apologize for entering this contest under an alias, and to assure all of you that no favoritism has been shown or will be shown if you decide to let me continue."

That was met with a few derisive snorts and a smattering of thoughtful nods from the other chefs. But Lara wasn't looking at anyone else. Her gaze was on Finn.

He recognized the apology in her expression, as well as the steely determination, when she added, "I'm asking for the opportunity to compete against you, but I'll understand whatever you decide."

"No! That's my vote," Ryder blurted out.

Tristan held up a hand. "Perhaps a secret ballot would be—"

"There's no need to waste more time," the big man complained. "Who's with me? Who else wants to see this poser gone for good?"

Not surprisingly, Angel's hand shot up, as did the hands of two other female chefs.

"I do, too," another man said, stepping forward. He cast an apologetic glance in Lara's direction. "Sorry, but I've gotten passed over for other positions because of nepotism."

Nepotism was hardly an issue in this situation. If anything, her relationship to her father put her at a disadvantage, Finn thought. But she didn't argue with the guy. She didn't even blink. She accepted his opinion with an almost imperceptible nod.

"All right, that makes five. Anyone else?" Tristan asked. "Speak now or forever hold your peace."

"I think she should stay." Flo Gimball rested her fists on a pair of ample hips. "Y'all are being way too hard on

Lara. She earned her place here just like the rest of us. It shouldn't matter who her daddy is."

The young chef named Kirby echoed Flo's sentiments. Lara gained the support of three more chefs after that, bringing the vote to five in favor. It all came down to Finn. A hush fell over the room. He felt Ryder's animosity. It rippled from the man the way heat wafted off the asphalt in August.

"Like we don't know how he's going to vote," Ryder muttered, resting his hand on the hilt of the fillet knife that was hooked to his belt. If this were a contest to decide who was the most intimidating chef, he would win it hands down. But it was about cooking.

"Afraid to compete against her?" Finn asked mildly.

"No way!"

"Good." He glanced at Lara as he told Tristan, "She stays."

Lara was relieved to be back in the competition. More than relieved—she was excited. As well as about a dozen other emotions that fizzed and popped in her mind like bubbles in a celebratory glass of champagne. It was a lot to process. For the past couple of weeks she'd been on a roller coaster, seated in the first car with a faulty safety bar as it had plunged into oblivion, only to rise and plunge again.

It had been one crazy ride…in more ways than one.

Finn.

Feelings she'd never experienced before when it came to a man bubbled up inside her and threatened to boil over. It didn't help that when she tried to catch his eye now, he wouldn't look at her.

While his vote had determined she would compete, it was almost as if he didn't trust her.

There was no time now, but she wanted to explain.

Sunday, a mere hour after Finn dropped her at her door,

Tristan had called to summon her to the studio for a last-minute meeting with the network brass and the lawyers. She'd assumed the worst, especially since Tristan had been so tight-lipped on the phone. Was she being sued? All he would tell Lara was that she needed to sign some official forms. She'd walked into the meeting worried about the legal ramifications of her actions and walked out with her head all but spinning.

They weren't going to sue her. Better yet, Lara still had a shot at joining the other chefs in the studio for taping and competing on the televised program. No one would explain the network's change of heart or why it had taken nearly two weeks to make the decision they had. Indeed, no one would give her a straight answer when she asked what her father thought of the change. Tristan just kept pointing out that nothing was a done deal. Everything hinged on what her fellow competitors decided.

That caveat had succeeded in keeping her hopes in check overnight. She knew some and possibly a majority of the other chefs had to be happy with the idea of having one less person to compete against on the show. So, she'd remained on pins and needles until the votes were cast.

She was in!

Thanks to Finn.

She should be able to breathe easier now, but she couldn't. She wasn't sure how she felt about his vote being the reason she was allowed to compete, since she knew how much he wanted to win. Not just wanted, but how much he *needed* this victory. Nor could she be certain what his thoughts were either. His expression gave nothing away. It didn't help that since giving her return the thumbs-up, he hadn't said a word. Not to her, not to Tristan. Not even to Ryder, who'd been goading Finn with insults akin to the sous-chef remark he'd made the first day.

She supposed she couldn't blame Finn for giving her the

silent treatment. Technically, she'd done the same to him. He'd phoned her twice. She'd let both calls go to voice mail. And she hadn't returned either call.

In her defense, she hadn't known what to say and she didn't want to lie. At the meeting, the show's lawyers had requested that she sign a second confidentiality agreement. All of the competitors had had to sign one going in. Since the show was taped in advance, the document was to ensure they did not divulge the weekly eliminations and ultimate winner before the last episode aired.

This one, however, covered Sunday's meeting as well as the possibility of her return. She was to tell no one, to discuss their offer with no one.

She waited until he walked over to the coffeepot in the corner of the greenroom to approach him.

"Want a cup?" he asked as he finished pouring some for himself.

"Please." She nodded. He filled her cup and handed it to her. When he started to move away, she added meaningfully, "And thank you."

"Don't thank me," he replied. His tone was surprisingly terse. "Five other people wanted to let you continue."

"But you were the deciding vote," she said quietly. "Are you having regrets?"

Finn met her gaze. His eyes were stormy gray and narrowed in irritation. "That's not how I operate, Lara. I believe in being aboveboard."

"What's that supposed to mean?"

But he ignored her and continued. "You'll get your chance."

"That's all I could hope for."

"Give it your best shot. I'm not going to have anyone claim that I won by default. And, frankly, I plan to beat you. I'm not going to hold back."

"I expect nothing less," she replied. She was starting to feel offended, indignant.

"Good." He nodded. "Great. But I do have a question for you. When did all this go down? Before we...hooked up?"

Lara backed up a step, feeling almost as if Finn had slapped her.

"What are you implying?"

"I'm not implying anything." His shoulders lifted. "Just wondering."

Just wondering, my ass.

She knew he had trust issues, but still.

"You think I slept with you to get your vote? What, do you think I slept with Flo and the others, too?"

"You only needed six votes. There are more than six guys here," he pointed out with maddening nonchalance.

Anger warred with the pain his words caused. She decided she'd rather be ticked off than vulnerable. She set down the hot coffee since she was tempted to toss it in Finn's face. The words *Go to hell* were on the tip of her tongue. She opted for sarcasm instead.

"Ryder apparently forgot about our bargain."

She heard Finn's muffled curse as she walked away.

Block it out, she commanded. Forget about Finn, their amazing two weeks together and what she'd thought might be the start of something a little longer lived.

She was here to win, and her reasons for wanting to get to the final round hadn't changed.

CHAPTER FIFTEEN

Sear

FINN LISTENED WHILE Garrett St. John went over the rules, not only for the television audience who would be tuning in at some point, but for the contestants.

To accommodate Lara's presence in the competition, all of the tastings would be done blind. That meant that instead of the chefs explaining their dishes to the panel of judges, Garrett would do the honors.

It was hot under the set's lights, even though every now and then Finn caught a rush of cool air from one of the ducts overhead. He fought the urge to swipe the sleeve of his chef coat over his forehead and cast a discreet glance around at his competition. No one was smiling. Ryder's death-row grimace wasn't surprising. But even down-home Flo looked as if she could chew nails. They all had their game faces on today.

That included Lara, even though he could hardly bring himself to look at her. His temper had cooled enough since their exchange in the greenroom that Finn could admit accusing her of sleeping with the other male chefs on the show had been low. As for accusing her of sleeping with him to ensure his vote, he didn't want to believe it, but doubt nagged like a bad tooth.

Finn hated that since his divorce he was so damned

quick to distrust people, particularly women. And Lara was the first woman he'd allowed close. But the fact remained that he wanted to be clear on the timeline. What had Lara known and when? And why hadn't she returned his phone calls? That in particular seemed damning.

The studio was crowded with people. Garrett was introducing the competitors now. The cameras trained on each one while a pithy biography was read. When they got to Lara, her connection to Clifton had to be disclosed.

Finn gave the producers credit not only for covering their asses, but doing so in such a way as to court higher ratings.

After reading off Lara's résumé, which on its own was impressive, Garrett said, "Her name may sound familiar. Lara Dunham is Clifton Chesterfield's daughter. Some of you may think that makes her a shoo-in to win." He waited a beat while a camera zoomed in closer and then he smiled. "Not so.

"Her own father has made it known that he does not want her working in his restaurant. In fact, their estrangement is exactly why Clifton Chesterfield agreed to let *Executive Chef Challenge* do his hiring this season. Here is what her father had to say in a previously taped segment after it was revealed that one of the show's contestants was, in fact, his daughter, who had entered under an alias."

Finn and the rest of them could hear the audio, although they couldn't see the actual feed. As it played, a dozen cameras panned to Lara.

"Lara is a disappointment. She was given the finest education, training and culinary opportunities a chef can have and she threw them aside."

"She works as a food stylist," Garrett could be heard saying on the tape. "From what I've been told, she is rather respected in her field."

"She can make food look appetizing. Despite all of her

training, however, she is no chef, which is why I won't hire her."

"Is that the only reason?"

"Are you are referring to the fact that she was married to Jeffrey Dunham?" Clifton thundered ominously.

Garrett was undeterred. "It had to have been a slap in the face. Your feud with Dunham was very well-known."

There was a pause. A long one. In that gap of silence, Finn swore he could hear Lara breathing.

"Her decision to wed that…alleged food critic certainly didn't help our relationship. It goes to show how impulsive and immature she is. Neither characteristic is what I am looking for in an executive chef."

"In fairness, that was six years ago," St. John said. "And the marriage didn't last."

"Exactly."

"As I understand it, the two of you haven't spoken since then."

"That's because I have nothing to say to her."

"And if she wins?" Garrett asked.

"I'm not worried about that," her father said on the tape.

"No?"

Clifton made a scoffing sound. From the corner of his eye, Finn saw Lara flinch.

"Lara won't win. Ultimately, she doesn't have what it takes to be a great chef. And only a great chef will run my kitchen."

Lara's face was nearly as pale as her white coat by the time the interview ended. While it had played, Garrett, followed by several more cameramen, had made their way over to her workstation.

"Those are some harsh words that your father had for you, Chef Dunham," the host said.

"He's entitled to his opinion," she replied stoically.

Apparently, her response—or lack of one—wasn't what the show's producers were after, so St. John tried again.

"Still, it must be extremely difficult to hear him say that you don't have what it takes to win."

Sympathy infused Garrett's tone, but the emotion was manufactured, as proved by the fact that he asked for a second and then a third take before he felt he had conveyed the appropriate amount.

"He's wrong," Lara finally got to respond.

"Let's get on with it already." Ryder's complaint carried from the other side of the set.

Finn and the others were in complete agreement. Garrett and the people associated with the show were lapping up the added drama, but the chefs just wanted to cook.

Lara included.

Her nerves were palpable when they finally got under way. She nibbled the inside of her cheek. Under the set's hot lights, perspiration dotted her brow. She glanced over at Finn. It was on the tip of his tongue to assure her she would do well. He didn't. He couldn't.

"Chefs," St. John began. With a dramatic sweep of his hand, he indicated the table before him. "These are the cards you have been dealt."

And so it began.

Lara's heart was beating fast and loud, pounding in her ears and making it difficult to hear. She glanced at Finn. He stood with his legs shoulder-width apart, his hands on his hips. His eyes were narrowed and his jaw clenched. He looked more like he was gearing up for hand-to-hand combat than food preparation. She felt the same way.

Especially now.

She had two goals today. One was to stay in the competition. She already knew what it felt like to have to leave. She didn't plan to exit early again. Her second goal was more personal than professional. She planned to make sure her food earned higher marks than Finn's.

She was so angry with him, so…hurt. And, dammit, that just wouldn't do. So, she channeled her irritation into determination as she eyed the three oversize rectangles on the tabletop.

Garrett was saying, "The cards have been dealt, chefs. The first card will be for the amount of time you have to prepare your dish." He turned it over with a flourish. "Twenty minutes."

Twenty minutes!

She heard Finn suck in a breath. Across the kitchen studio, Ryder let loose an oath that would have to be edited out later. Dear God, Lara hoped that the second card, which would tell them the kind of dish they needed to prepare, would not be an entrée. Working up a main course with any depth of flavor would be damned hard in so short a time.

"And now for the second card."

She nearly sagged with relief when the card read *Appetizer.* Given the vast assortment of ingredients in the fridge and pantry, she could pull off a tasty and creative hors d'oeuvre in twenty minutes. Finn could, too. Asparagus spears wrapped in prosciutto and phyllo dough sprang to mind. Had it really been just over a week ago since the two of them sat in his cousin's pub and enjoyed drinks and finger food while attraction sizzled and the promise of a relationship had simmered? She glanced over and their gazes met.

She recognized distrust when she saw it. Still, seeing it reflected in Finn's eyes—the same eyes that, less than twenty-four hours earlier, had regarded her with affection that had the potential to become so much more… Well, it cut to the bone.

Garrett's voice tugged her back to the present when he revealed the third card.

"And your celebrity judge for this round, chefs, is Robin Falconi. Ms. Falconi is the executive chef at Mateo's in La Jolla, California. She is the author of three cookbooks on Southwestern cuisine."

"Southwestern cuisine," Lara repeated half under her breath.

The smart thing would be to steer clear of that type of fare. Unfortunately, playing it safe in this competition held its own set of perils.

"Not your forte?" Finn asked. His voice was barely above a whisper. Even so, it held the edge of challenge.

She shook her head before she could think better of it. Revealing a weakness was never a good idea, especially to an opponent who'd already managed to deal her a nearly lethal blow.

"Gee, that's too bad," he added.

"As I recall, you're not exactly an expert on that style of cooking either."

"You don't know what I'm capable of."

She nodded, put a hand over the tiny microphone attached to her shirt. "I totally agree with you on that score. I thought I knew, but… Well, you proved me wrong today."

"Don't." Finn covered his mike, too. "Don't even go there. You're the one—"

He broke off as a big, fuzzy microphone lowered from overhead.

"Chefs," Garrett said. "Your time starts in three…two… one…"

A buzzer sounded, echoing on the set. Lara swore she felt it vibrate through her bones. All twelve chefs took off like a shot in the direction of the refrigerator and pantry. Finn was behind her one moment, ahead of her the next thanks to his longer stride.

"On your left, chef," he called as he passed.

He might be angry with her, but he remained civil. Ryder,

however, didn't bother with courtesy. Putting a hand on the small of her back, he shoved her out of the way. Lara banged her hip on the sharp edge of a prep station. She glanced up to see that Finn had stopped.

"All right?" he asked.

Because his concern caused her heart to ache and vulnerability to creep back in, she snapped, "Don't worry about me."

"That's right. You know how to look after yourself."

Their exchange took only a few seconds, but that was long enough that by the time they reached the pantry, the spice rack and selection of fresh vegetables had been picked over. Ryder was already starting back to his station, his arms filled with a couple of different kinds of lettuce and all of the ingredients to make vinaigrette.

A salad. Really?

Finn apparently reached the same conclusion.

"That had better be one hell of a dressing," he said.

Lara moved a bin of mixed peppers and spied a bowl containing half a dozen avocados shoved to the back of the shelves. Either it had been overlooked, or several of the chefs had opted to play it safe and not go the Southwestern route.

Before she could grab a few of the avocados, Finn snatched up the entire bowl.

"Hey!" she hollered. "Do you really need all of them?"

"Need?" He glanced at the bowl, which held six, and shook his head. "No. I'm figuring one, possibly two."

But he made no move to put the bowl back.

"You aren't going to share, are you?" She snorted.

"This is a competition, Lara," he reminded her needlessly.

"So, all's fair in love and war?"

She regretted the words as soon as they were out. His

lips twisted with what passed for a smile, but his eyes glittered as hard as stone.

"I could ask the same thing," he shot back.

She swallowed, but notched up her chin and rallied. "Go ahead and hoard ingredients. I get it."

His eyes narrowed. "What do you get?"

"You're afraid if we make the same thing mine will taste better."

Rough laughter erupted. "Reverse psychology. Pathetic."

She arched one brow and said nothing.

"Here. Knock yourself out." He reached into the bowl and took the two ripest avocados before handing it to her.

Lara didn't have time to be relieved. As for saying thank-you, she didn't get the chance. Finn had already turned and started back to his workstation with a couple of cameramen in tow. She grabbed spices, heirloom tomatoes and a can of black beans, as well as a couple of dried spices. Just before hurrying back to her station, she grabbed a couple of yams. She'd decided to make a hash of sorts, updating the flavor profile with unexpected ingredients and spices.

By the time she returned to her prep table, nearly three minutes had passed.

Finn was already busy at his cutting board. His avocados were pitted and peeled, and he was slicing a rolled-up bundle of fresh basil leaves into thin ribbons. His movements were deft, fluid. A day earlier, she would have admired his skill with a knife. There was something to be said for a gorgeous guy who knew how to make a chiffonade. But his words in the greenroom made her resent the traitorous tug of longing she felt low in her belly.

"Looking to see how it's done?" he asked without glancing up.

"Just making sure you're not going to cut off a finger. Blood doesn't pair well with the first course I have in mind."

"I know what I'm doing. I haven't nicked myself since culinary school."

"Then maybe you're due," she said.

She'd been teasing. So, Lara felt horrible when a moment later she heard his ripe curse and glanced back to find him gripping his hand with a white towel. A splotch of bright crimson bloomed on the fabric.

"Oh, my God, are you—"

"I'm fine," he bit out.

Somehow he managed to bandage his finger and don a latex glove before the host's voice came over the loudspeaker to announce, "Chefs, you have fifteen minutes left to prepare your appetizers."

For the remaining quarter of an hour, neither of them spoke. Nor did they make eye contact until the buzzer sounded and time was called.

Lara stepped back from the prep table, both hands held aloft, and eyed her mixture of avocados, tomatoes, black beans and sautéed yams. She gave it an A for taste. Cumin and smoky paprika lingered on her tongue from the bite she'd sampled just prior to plating. The food stylist in her, however, wasn't pleased with the overall presentation. The crisp white shallow bowls were the right choice, but she should have added a garnish, perhaps a sprig of something green and leafy. Or maybe even put the hash inside a leaf of bib lettuce first. It was too late now, of course.

She glanced over at Finn's dish. Even though they'd both used avocado, they'd gone different directions. While she'd detoured to the Southwest, his inspiration clearly had come from Italy.

The plate of bow-tie pasta was covered in a rich sauce into which he had incorporated the avocado. *Good call*, she thought. The portion size was perfect as a first course. She would have plated it differently, but given that Finn had been working injured, she gave him credit for finishing ahead of the clock. One of the competitors hadn't, she realized, after a couple of young production assistants came around with a cart to collect the plates. The fact that one of that chef's plates was missing the sauce on his appetizer wasn't an automatic dismissal, but it certainly tilted the odds.

In the greenroom, the chefs flopped down onto the various chairs and couches. The only seats that remained unoccupied were on the couch next to Ryder. Lara decided she would rather stand. She picked a spot next to the coffeemaker and leaned against the wall. She needed the extra support to remain upright. Her head was still spinning, both from the competition and from her fight with Finn.

Let it go, she kept telling herself, but to no avail. Her heart was too bruised for that. For the first time in a long time, she'd let down her guard. She'd thought…

"That was tougher than I expected it to be," one of the chefs said, drawing her attention.

"Twenty minutes!" another shouted. "It felt more like two."

"I know! I swear I just got started and they were calling time," added the chef who had failed to finish plating on time. After which he lamented, "I'm as good as gone."

"It ain't over till it's over," Finn said.

Lara glanced over to find him staring at her. Staring, not glaring. Still, his expression was a long way from warm. He'd discarded the latex glove. His injured left hand had been rebandaged and was now cradled in his right.

She walked over to where he stood and asked, "How bad is it?"

"I'm fine."

"Maybe you should have the show's doctor look at it."

He shook his head. He appeared more wounded than his hand when he told her, "I've survived worse."

CHAPTER SIXTEEN

Blend on high

IT WAS SEVERAL more hours before the contestants learned the identity of the chef who would be the first to go home. It was the one who had failed to finish all of his plates in the allotted twenty minutes.

Ryder had scored in the bottom three with his unimaginative mixed-greens salad. He wasn't happy about it. He was especially unhappy to learn that Lara had scored higher. In fact, Lara's creative take on hash had put her in the top three along with Kirby and Finn.

Finn's Italian dish had scored the highest of all with the judges. He should have been ecstatic with his showing. He should have felt vindicated, given all of the lies his ex-wife had circulated about him and his ability to concoct recipes with interesting flavor profiles. But late that evening as he let himself into his apartment after one of the longest and most grueling days of his life, all he could think about was Lara.

Finn was confused and hurt and he was still angry. He just wasn't sure whom he was angry with. Lara? Her father? The show? Or himself?

He twisted off the cap from a bottle of beer and plunked down on the couch in his sparsely furnished apartment. The place seemed especially empty now. As he ruminated over the day's events, the telephone rang. Picking it up, he realized he had nearly a dozen voice-mail messages waiting to be played back.

"Hello?" he said into the receiver.

Kate was on the other end of the line.

"Finally!" his sister shouted by way of a greeting. "Where have you been? You haven't answered your cell all day."

"I turned it off for the show." And he'd never turned it back on after leaving the studio. "Is anything wrong?"

"Is anything wrong?" she repeated, followed by a loud scoffing noise that had him pulling the receiver away from his ear. "Jeez, Finn. We're all here at Mom and Dad's dying to find out what happened today. You promised you would call after filming."

He set the beer down so he could rub his eyes. "Right. Sorry."

"Well? Quit keeping us in suspense. Are you still on the show or what?" Kate all but screamed the question.

In the background, he could hear his mother say, "Good heavens, Katie, don't put it like that. You make it sound like we have no faith in him."

A second later, she was on the line and the echo made it clear he'd been put on speaker.

"We're proud of you, Finn. No matter what happened today. You know that."

He smiled in spite of his foul mood. But once again he found himself thinking of Lara and the way she'd looked as Garrett played back the interview with her father. As proud as Finn's parents would be of him even in failure, nothing she did measured up to her father's unrealistic expectations.

"I'm still on the show, Mom. In fact, I had the highest score in today's round."

A flurry of excited squeals greeted his news.

"I knew it!" his mother replied.

"Have you told Lara yet?" Kate asked.

"Actually, I didn't need to. She was there today."

"She came to watch you?"

"I didn't think they allowed outsiders on the set," his mother said.

Kristy wanted to know, "Can we come and watch next time?"

He reached for his beer and took a gulp as he waited for the speculation to die down.

"She didn't come to watch me. She came…she came to compete. The network agreed to let her back on the show."

He didn't mention that the decision had hinged on his vote. Nor did he divulge the harsh words that had passed between the pair of them afterward.

His sisters were once again talking over each other, peppering him with questions. His mother, however, cut to the heart of the matter. He heard a click and the girls' voices receded. He was off the speaker and pretty sure that his mother was now moving to a more private location to continue the conversation. She was an expert at reading between the lines.

"You're upset."

"No, Mom—"

"You are. What's happened?" she asked in a tone that told him she didn't want to argue. She wanted an explanation.

He sighed.

"I saw her just yesterday…. Hell, we've practically spent every day of the past two weeks together, and she never mentioned…" He took another pull on his beer. The sour taste in his mouth lingered nonetheless.

"She knew and didn't tell you?"

"I—I'm not sure. But I called her last night and this morning and she didn't return either call."

"Okay, back up a minute. You said you're not sure what she knew. Did you ask her?"

"Not exactly. But like I said, I called her last night and this morning. I find it a little odd, not to mention suspect, that she didn't call me back," he added, feeling riled up and once again justified in his anger. "And then, today, when she walked into the greenroom…she looked…guilty."

Finn drained his beer.

"But you didn't let her explain?"

"Mom—"

"Do you like this woman, Griffin?"

He scraped at the edge of the label on his empty beer bottle and said nothing.

"Okay, I'll answer for you. You do. In fact, I think you like her a lot."

"We only just met. There's a lot I don't know about her." He grunted and got up from the couch. While he went to the kitchen for another beer, he added, "In fact, she lied to me the first time we met. She told me her name was Lara Smith."

"Yes, I remember you mentioning that to me. And *why* did she lie about that? Hmm?"

"Okay, she said it was to get on the show without anyone knowing who her father is, but there's a pattern here, Mom," he insisted.

He twisted off the beer's cap and tossed it in the direction of the trash can. It missed and pinged off a cabinet door before rolling across the floor.

"Did you ever think maybe you see a pattern because what Sheryl and Cole did to you has made it difficult for you to trust people, especially people you have feelings for?"

"Maybe," he allowed.

He knew better than to argue with his mother. He was guaranteed to lose. Besides, she had a point, one that he had already considered. But the gap between what his head recognized and what his heart felt was not easily spanned.

"Do yourself a favor, Griffin, and give her the benefit of the doubt until the two of you can sit down and have a proper conversation."

He hung up agreeing that he would, but when he went to bed that night, he still had not called Lara.

The week passed, and with it two more rounds of competition that saw another pair of chefs sent packing. Ryder stepped up his game and managed to stay out of the bottom three both times. Meanwhile, Finn and Lara remained in the top tier. Already, they had been targeted as the two to beat. As such, they found themselves largely ostracized in the greenroom. Even Flo and Kirby now kept their chitchat to a minimum. Ryder, of course, was happy to speak to them, as long as he was slinging insults. Lara had learned to tune him out. More difficult to tolerate, however, was the silence from Finn. It was deafening.

Every now and then, she would catch him watching her. But then his jaw would clench and his gaze would harden before sliding away.

She missed him. Deeply. And she mourned what might have been. She'd never admitted her feelings to him. She hadn't even admitted them to herself. But she knew she'd been falling in love. And that realization, even unspoken, made her ache.

The days were long, the schedule grueling. While the actual cooking took up very little time, they spent hours at the studio, taping interview segments after the fact in which they discussed culinary techniques, recipes and ingredient choices, and even talked a little smack about their fellow competitors. Lara kept her comments to a minimum, even though the producers made it clear that tension and drama made for better ratings.

Tension. There was plenty of that between her and Finn.

The second week ended. Three more chefs were sent home, Kirby among them, bringing the number to six. On the following Monday, after another casualty was announced, Lara was outside waiting for a cab when she spied Finn exiting the building.

They still weren't talking, but they'd brokered a truce of sorts. While Ryder and some of the other chefs hoarded ingredients, Finn always shared and vice versa.

Their gazes met and he nodded in quasi-greeting.

"That was a tough one," she remarked.

"I can't believe you pulled off such a complex entrée in forty minutes."

A complete sentence as well as a compliment. The surprise must have shown on her face, because he added, "I've never doubted your ability in the kitchen, Lara. See you tomorrow."

She swallowed hard as she watched him walk away. No, she thought, he'd just doubted *her*.

By the final week of competition, four chefs remained: Lara, Finn, Angel and Ryder.

"You're going down," Ryder assured her in the green-room before the day's competition began. "You've stayed on too long already."

"We'll see," she replied mildly.

At her prep station half an hour later, she swore under her breath when Garrett announced they would have thirty minutes to prepare a dessert, and the celebrity chef who would be helping to score their dishes just so happened to be a renowned pastry chef.

"This sucks," she heard Finn mutter.

"If you know how to make the shortbread your mom served at her party, you'll be staying," she murmured.

He glanced sideways, looking surprised and, she wanted to believe, grateful.

Lara wound up making an apricot tartlet with cinnamon-infused whipped cream.

"Your crust looks good," Finn remarked after time was called.

"I'm worried it's not flaky enough."

"It's fine." He reached over and gave her hand a squeeze. "And thanks for the suggestion."

He nodded toward his plates, where he'd turned shortbread cookies into sandwiches with a creamy raspberry filling and dipped one side in dark chocolate.

"I didn't suggest all that." She squeezed his hand back. "And nice plating, by the way."

He'd included some fresh raspberries and a sprig of mint.

Half of his mouth rose. "I just asked myself, 'What would Lara do?'"

A little while later, after their desserts had been scored by the judges, the chefs once again stood at their stations, hands clasped in front of them, as Garrett read off the name of the latest casualty.

"Angel, I'm sorry, but you have been eliminated," the host said, tilting his head to one side in feigned sympathy.

Under the set's bright lights, the woman's eyes glittered, not with tears, but with pure hatred.

"Blind tasting, my ass! I know what's going on here." She flipped Garrett her middle finger before pointing the neighboring digit in Lara's direction. "We all know the judges have been told which dishes are hers so that she will wind up winning."

"That's not true," Garrett replied mildly, although the complexion under his salon tan paled a little. "All of the judges commented that your ice cream was neither the right consistency nor sweet enough."

Trying to reason with Angel now, however, was like trying to reason with a charging bull. She saw red and wasn't about to stop until she had gored someone. She spouted out half a dozen more accusations, accompanied by language that a longshoreman would have hesitated to use. All of those four-letter words were going to have to be bleeped out before the segment aired on television. Fifteen minutes into her tirade, security was called to the set.

As two uniformed guards escorted Angel off the set, she warned Lara, "Watch your back, bitch!"

"That was unpleasant," Garrett said, adjusting the French cuffs on his designer shirt.

Since several cameras were trained on Lara, waiting to catalog her reaction, she remained stoic. The network wanted drama, but she would be damned if she would provide any more of it than she already had.

After that, the chefs were sent home early. Angel's unbecoming exit had cast a pall over the set. None of the contestants, judges or even the crew felt much like continuing with business as usual.

Lara's plan was to go home, pour herself a glass of wine, draw a hot bath and then soak in it until her skin was shriveled and prunelike. She was surprised when she spotted Finn milling about near the curb, especially since she'd given him a good fifteen minutes of lead time.

"Waiting for a cab?" she inquired.

"Actually, I was waiting for you. I have something I've been meaning to say."

"Now?" Because she was still feeling raw from Angel's scene in the studio, she wasn't sure she had the fortitude for another confrontation. And, despite their pleasant exchange at the prep station, she didn't trust Finn. He'd pulled the rug out from under her once already. So, she said, "Other than today, you've barely said a word to me since the filming started, and now you want to talk?"

"I do." Finn tucked his hands into the front pockets of his jeans and regarded her with the very eyes that had been haunting her dreams.

"Can we go someplace, maybe sit down and have coffee?"

She wanted to say no. To protect that broken heart that was far from becoming mended. But more than anything, she wanted Finn, so she agreed.

"Isadora's?"

Finn waited till they'd ordered coffee and biscotti to begin. Just in case she told him to go to hell, he wanted to savor her company.

"Lara, about what I said that day in the greenroom." His voice cracked from nerves, forcing him to clear his throat before he could go on. "I was surprised and angry. Trust, well, it isn't my strong suit."

"I know that, Finn. And I know why."

"I—I should have asked for an explanation before jumping to conclusions."

Her eyes widened and she blinked before nodding slowly. "Is that what you're doing now? Are you asking me for an explanation?"

"No." He shook his head. "My mom told me right away that I owed you the benefit of the doubt until we talked."

"Your mom said that?" A smile tugged briefly at the corners of her mouth.

"Yes, she did."

"I haven't exactly felt as if you've withheld judgment," she reminded him.

"I know. I've had a lot of thinking to do. Not about you as much as the way I treated you." He reached over and gave her hand a squeeze. "When you…when you care about someone the way I care about you, you don't just give them the benefit of the doubt, Lara. You don't need explanations."

"Oh."

He squeezed her hand again, but this time he didn't let go. He held on firmly when he added, "Lara, I know we just met, but I've only felt this way about one other woman in my life. I guess I let the past cloud my judgment." He shook his head. "Guess? I know I did. No excuse for it. I screwed up. Big-time. And I'm sorry. Give me another chance. It's a lot to ask, I know. But I promise you this— I'll never doubt you again."

She blinked, looking momentarily undone by what he was telling her. Since Finn knew the feeling, he took that as a good sign.

She turned over the hand he'd been holding and twined her fingers through his.

"For the record, other than my choice of career, I'm nothing like Sheryl, Finn. I will never betray you the way she did."

"I know. I guess my head just needed to catch up to my heart. So, do you forgive me?"

"Yes. I've been miserable without you."

"I've been miserable, too." But he smiled now as the pressure that had been building in his chest finally gave way.

They went to his apartment since it was closer.

Lara knew a moment of regret that she wasn't wearing anything spectacularly sexy beneath her clothes. No lacy demi-cup bra or racy thong. Plain white bra and a pair of boy-cut panties whose only bow to femininity or playfulness was their color: hot pink.

But then, when she'd set out that morning, she hadn't planned to be seduced and eager to return the favor.

"Just to be clear, I still intend to win," she told him as he lowered her onto the couch.

"That's fine."

"Yeah."

"Uh-huh. Because I intend to beat you."

"Okay." She nipped his lower lip with her teeth before asking, "What do you think about fraternizing with the enemy?"

"I'm all for it."

CHAPTER SEVENTEEN

Add garnish

"AND THEN THERE were three," Garrett announced in an ominous tone at the start of the next round of competition. "Only Chef Dunham, Chef Westbrook and Chef Surkovski remain. Today's competition will determine who will go head-to-head in the high-stakes finale."

"God, I hope it's not dessert again," Finn muttered.

"Same here." Lara sent him a smile.

It was the smile that bolstered his mood, even after the cards were dealt. The good news? They didn't have to make a dessert. They were tasked with creating an entrée. The bad news—they had just twenty minutes to do that.

Ryder's oath upon hearing the time allotment echoed in the studio.

"Oh, God!" Lara groaned. "Another twenty-minute entrée."

So far, that had happened only once in the competition, but it was enough to shake her confidence. That time, she'd failed to completely finish, leaving off the sauce in her haste to beat the clock. The combination of spices in her shrimp dish, however, was imaginative enough to keep her from being eliminated.

"You've got this," Finn told her, even though he was unnerved, too. "Or did you come this far to lose before the final round?"

Her spine stiffened as he'd hoped it would. "I'm not going anywhere."

"That's my girl," he murmured under his breath.

If he could have kissed her then, he would have. But he had to settle for knowing he would be able to kiss her later, in private. At which time he planned to engage a lot more than her mouth.

Finn decided to do a Spanish twist on an Italian dish, by making pasta carbonara using chorizo sausage. He just barely finished in time and the plating... Well, it wasn't pretty.

Lara, meanwhile, had seasoned scallops with lime zest, sea salt and freshly ground black pepper, which she'd then sautéed in garlic butter before placing them over a bed of mixed greens. She'd run out of time to make a dressing, so she'd made do with fresh lime juice and a drizzle of extra virgin olive oil. A couple of grilled slices of French bread provided both the starch and the texture. Visually, her dish was gorgeous.

"I knew you could do it," he whispered.

"Thanks for the pep talk, by the way."

"Anytime."

"Looks like Ryder went with flank steak and a basic salad. I don't see any starch on his plate," she noted.

"Not exactly imaginative," Finn replied.

The judges didn't think so either.

"Chef Surkovski," Garrett intoned gravely. "You will not be moving on in the competition."

Ryder cursed and, with a sweep of one tattooed forearm, sent all of the utensils, bowls and bottles of oil crashing to the tiled floor.

"This is bull! I'm going to sue. By the time I'm done, I'll own both this network and the Chesterfield," he threatened.

Ryder left the set the same way Angel had: escorted by security guards.

"The finale is fixed!" he screamed just before the door closed behind him.

Fixed? Finn saw it as fated, especially after he ran into Lara's father in the elevator on the way up the last day of the competition.

The older man didn't scowl or make a nasty remark. Instead, he nodded in greeting as the doors slid closed.

Still wary, Finn nodded back and tucked his hands into his pockets. As the elevator rose, he kept his gaze trained above the doors on the lit floor numbers. He expected the ride to be accomplished in silence, so he was surprised when Clifton cleared his throat and began to speak.

"You got your wish, young man. Are you regretting it now?"

"I'm afraid I don't know what you mean."

"I called the network after you and my daughter came by the restaurant that day."

Finn gaped at the older man in surprise. "You mean *you're* responsible for her returning to the show?"

Clifton's laughter was dry. "From what I understand, you were responsible for that."

Lara's father was right, but...

"You agreed to give her a chance to compete. Why?"

"I paid for her education and training."

"So, you let her back on to satisfy your curiosity?" Finn wasn't buying it.

"Are you always this outspoken, young man?"

"Only when I know I'm right."

Dry laughter rang out again before Clifton sobered. "It may not seem like it from where you're standing, but I've always wanted the best for Lara."

"What she wants is your approval and your love."

"I may not have gone about it the way other fathers do, but I...I love my daughter."

Present tense.

"Have you told her that, Mr. Chesterfield? She needs to hear it."

They reached the network's floor as he said it. The doors opened and Clifton stepped out. For a moment, Finn thought the older man wasn't going to answer, but then he turned.

"I will. No matter who wins today...I will."

Garrett St. John dealt the cards and then flipped them over one by one.

"Chefs, you have forty minutes to make an entrée. Given the amount of time, our judges will be expecting something fabulous. I suggest you make good use of the pantry items.

"As you know, the tasting will be done blind, and, since this is the final round of competition, the guest judge is the one and only Clifton Chesterfield.

"Whoever wins today will be awarded a one-year contract as the executive chef of the Chesterfield's kitchen. Best of luck to you both." Garrett pointed to the oversize clock mounted on the wall. "And your time starts *now*!"

Finn's pulse took off like a jackrabbit even before his feet started to move. He knew what he had to do. He was going to lose the competition to Lara. It wasn't the first thing he'd lost to her. The woman already had his heart. He loved her enough that he wanted to ensure that she got the job at her father's restaurant. After his discussion with Clifton in the elevator, Finn was certain it was just the fix their fractured father-daughter relationship needed. Finn would find another way to rebuild his own career. Being a personal chef wasn't a bad thing. He could continue as he had been, socking away money, biding his time. And he had Lara.

Lara.

Nerves weren't the only thing making his heart beat unsteadily.

What was it his mom had always told him? You know you love someone when their happiness is more important than your own.

That was definitely the case here.

Lara glanced over at Finn. They'd returned from the pantry with their ingredients. She was going with blackened salmon. Her father detested blackened fish. That was why she was doing it. She planned to lose.

Finn needed the fresh start winning would provide. She wanted him to have the job at the Chesterfield. It was enough that she'd made it this far. It was enough that her father realized she was capable and skilled in the kitchen. And apparently, he did, because when she'd passed him in the studio on her way to her workstation, he'd not only made eye contact but also actually wished her luck.

"You haven't seasoned your rice," Finn murmured.

"What?"

He nudged the bowl of sea salt closer.

Lara nodded, but she didn't add any to the pot.

Finn was making fish, too. He'd gone with sea bass and, apparently recalling what she'd told him about her father's preparation preference, he'd put it on the grill.

It had been on there for several minutes already and he hadn't turned it.

"You might want to check your fish," she mumbled.

"It's fine."

"It needs to be flipped."

But Finn shook his head and insisted, "Not yet."

And so it went as the clock counted down the remaining time. Each of them reminding the other of things they needed to do or things they had left out.

When the buzzer sounded and they both stepped back with hands aloft, the dishes the judges would taste looked as if they had been prepared by first-year culinary students.

Or so the affable Garrett St. John quipped.

"I think nerves got the best of both of our contestants this round," he said.

In the greenroom, Lara grabbed a bottle of water from the mini-fridge and twisted off the cap. She downed half of it in a few gulps. Cooking badly was harder work than cooking well.

"What was that?" Finn asked mildly.

"Well, it was supposed to be blackened salmon and rice pilaf. It wasn't my best effort," she admitted.

"No kidding."

"Hey, you had an off day, too."

"Exactly. It should have been a cakewalk for you to beat me."

"Finn?"

Folding his arms over his chest, he backtracked then. "You know what I mean. I was...struggling."

Math wasn't her forte, but Lara was quite capable of putting two and two together.

"Yes, I think I do know what you mean." She recapped the water and studied him. "And I'm not sure whether I want to slap you for trying to throw—"

"I didn't throw—"

"Let me finish."

"Okay, you were going to slap me." He smiled.

"No, I was saying I didn't *know* whether I wanted to slap you for trying to throw the competition or kiss you!"

"If I get a vote, I choose the latter," Finn said.

She burst out laughing. "Dammit, Finn! I wanted you to win."

"So you left the salt out of your very unimaginative pilaf on purpose," he said.

"Among other acts of self-sabotage." At his questioning gaze, she admitted, "My father would rather eat a fast-food hamburger than blackened fish."

Finn's brows pulled together. "Why did you do that? You had a real shot at winning."

"So did you." She smiled. "I guess neither one of us wanted it as badly as we did at the start."

They reached for one another at the same time. When the greenroom's door opened several minutes later, they were still kissing. Even after Tristan clapped his hands together several times, they took their time drawing apart.

"You're wanted on the set," the young man told them.

"What do you think is going to happen?" Lara asked Finn.

"I don't know. But whatever happens, I want you to know something." He grabbed her hand, pulled her to a stop. "I love you, Lara."

"I love you, too."

EPILOGUE

Serves two

"TABLE TWENTY WANTS to see you, chef," the hostess said.

Lara sampled the cauliflower puree and nodded to the sous-chef before heading out to the Chesterfield's packed dining room.

Finn grinned as she approached. He was having dinner with her father.

It had been six months since the *Executive Chef Challenge* ended in the program's first-ever tie. Lara suspected that Clifton had intended that, since he couldn't be sure whose dish was whose.

He'd hired both of them, making them coexecutive chefs. Over the past several months, he and Lara had cobbled together a relationship that while far from perfect, was heading in that direction.

"You wanted to see me?" she asked her father.

"Actually, Finn did."

She smiled at the man she loved before noting his plate of untouched food. "Is something wrong?"

"There's something in my pasta."

"What do you mean…?"

She leaned closer to inspect it and her eyes rounded when she spied the something in question. It wasn't in Finn's pasta. Rather, it was on the side of the plate.

"Oh, my God! That's an…an…"

"An engagement ring."

The diamond was dazzling, but not more so than the man who now reached for her hand.

"I've just had a long talk with your father, Lara."

"Finn…"

But it was her father who spoke. "I trust this man with my restaurant. Still, I wasn't sure I trusted him with you. But he's proved himself these past several months. So, I'm giving him—I'm giving *both* of you—my blessing."

Tears blurred her vision. "Dad…"

"I love you, Lara." The words still didn't come easily to her father, but she knew he meant them.

"I love you, too."

Clifton cleared his throat then and his signature bluster returned. "Well, are you going to propose, young man?"

Finn grinned. "Oh, yeah."

"In my day, we got down on bended knee."

Lara tucked away her grin. Finn, meanwhile, took the suggestion without any quibbling. In full view of the rest of the restaurant's patrons, he got down on one knee. "I want to marry you, Lara."

It wasn't a question, exactly, but that was okay. Because as far as Lara was concerned, the kiss she gave him afterward served as her answer.

* * * * *

A sneaky peek at next month...

MODERN
tempted™

TRUE LOVE AND TEMPTATION!

My wish list for next month's titles...

In stores from 20th June 2014:

❏ Her Hottest Summer Yet – Ally Blake

❏ Who's Afraid of the Big Bad Boss?

— Nina Harrington

In stores from 4th July 2014:

❏ If Only... – Tanya Wright

❏ Only the Brave Try Ballet – Stefanie London

Available at WHSmith, Tesco, Asda, Eason, Amazon and Apple

Just can't wait?